Chocolate Rules
and the
Starship MEATLOAF

OTHER BOOKS YOU WILL ENJOY:

Ketchup Power and the Starship *Meatloaf,*
Jerry Piasecki

Teacher Vic Is a Vampire . . . Retired,
Jerry Piasecki

Laura for Dessert, *Jerry Piasecki*

The Sixth-Grade Mutants Meet the Slime,
Laura E. Williams

The Chocolate Touch, *Patrick Skene Catling*

Chocolate Fever, *Robert Kimmel Smith*

How to Eat Fried Worms, *Thomas Rockwell*

How to Fight a Girl, *Thomas Rockwell*

Chocolate Rules
and the
Starship MEATLOAF

Jerry Piasecki

A Yearling Book

Published by
Bantam Doubleday Dell Books for Young Readers
a division of
Bantam Doubleday Dell Publishing Group, Inc.
1540 Broadway
New York, New York 10036

ISBN: 0-440-41404-0

Printed in the United States of America

October 1997

10   9   8   7   6   5   4   3   2

OPM

For Amanda Piasecki and Wendy Rollin

CAST OF CHARACTERS

STARSHIP CREW
Captain Asher (Katherine)
Dr. Louis J. Kibbleman the 822nd (Louie)
Ketchupologist Arlonus Quick (Arlo)
Ketchupologist Theresa Oliver (Terri)
Android (D7)

CURRENT SIXTH-GRADERS
Kevin "BB" McKinney
Ellie Fergusan
Perry Hampton
Joyce Chapinski

FROM THE YEAR 6789 SIXTH-GRADERS
Bianca Kibbleman
Kurt Quick
Connie Quick
Pokey Asher

EVIL LUNCHROOM COOKS
Bertha Butterman
Beula Butterman

FORMER TIME TRAVELER, CURRENT TEACHER
Mr. Mueller

In the year 6789 a severe energy crisis struck Earth, threatening the very existence of humankind. A couple of thousand years earlier, ketchup had been found to be the most powerful fuel source in the universe. Many centuries later, ketchup was replaced by artificial synthochup, cheaper if somewhat less tasty. Soon the recipe for real ketchup was lost.

All went well until it was discovered that synthochup actually destroyed the machinery, computers, weather domes, starships and really cool Lionel trains it powered. Only one hope remained if humans were to survive in an empowered state. One last working starship and one brave crew would have to journey back in time. Their mission was to retrieve the recipe for ketchup and then bake a sufficient number of meatloaves to hold enough of the highly unstable fuel for a return trip to the future. Dr. Louis J. Kibbleman the 822nd, Captain Asher and ketchupologists Arlonus Quick and Theresa Oliver volunteered. They were joined by the android D7.

The journey back through time had unexpected consequences. Dr. Kibbleman, Arlonus and Theresa aged in reverse during the journey. When they arrived in today's time they were all twelve-year-old sixth-graders. Captain Asher wasn't as lucky. She de-aged to five years old, becoming the only starship captain to still be in kindergarten.

Despite the worst efforts of evil lunchroom cooks Bertha and Beula Butterman, the crew and their friends from the current century succeeded in their mission. With undetected stowaways on board, they launched the Starship Meatloaf and headed back to the sixty-eighth century. This is their story.

ne

Day: Saturday
Time: 11:22 A.M.
Date: The Present

Light like the light from a thousand suns filled the Starship *Meatloaf*. The four crew members, four passengers and two stowaways all shut their eyes and drifted silently through space and time.

The mission had been a stunning success. The *Meatloaf* was returning to the future with the lost ingredients for the most powerful fuel source ever discovered . . . ketchup.

Sixth-graders Ellie Fergusan, Kevin "BB" McKinney, Joyce Chapinski and Perry Hampton had helped the mission achieve its happy ending and were now on a journey that would take them almost five thousand years into the future.

BB was the first to open his eyes. The light was beginning to fade, and he could make out the forms of his friends and of the time travelers he knew as five-year-old Katherine and twelve-year-olds Louie, Arlo and Terri Droid. He squinted and looked around the starship. The crew of the *Meatloaf* appeared changed. BB's observation was confirmed when Katherine, the kindergartner, rose from the captain's seat and stood almost six feet tall.

"Hi, BB." She winked and smiled. "We're almost there."

"Nice flying, Captain Asher."

BB turned at the sound of an adult male's voice. His eyes grew to the size of beach balls as Arlo unbuckled and stood up. Louie and Terri rose from their seats a moment later. All of them were now fully grown and definitely adults. Their shirtsleeves ended just past their elbows. Their pant legs fell a few inches below their knees. And all their clothes were bursting at the seams.

Louie bent over to tie his shoe. The sound of splitting fabric filled the *Meatloaf*. "Maybe we'd better change," Louie, the former sixth-grader, said, covering his bottom with a clipboard.

"Uh, I think you already have." Ellie had opened her eyes and was nudging Joyce and Perry. "Hey, guys, I think you'd better see this."

"Doctor Louis J. Kibbleman at your service." Louie held the clipboard in place with one hand while waving to everyone with the other. "And I'd like you to meet Captain Asher and Ketchupologists First Class Theresa Oliver and Arlonus Quick."

"What's up, duds?" Arlonus said in the ancient tongue of the passengers. "Isn't the sixty-eighth century totally nippy?" Arlonus hadn't quite mastered the slang of the earlier era they had just left behind.

Theresa stretched her legs, causing popping sounds to resound from her knees. "Ouch," she whispered, and massaged.

"Are you okay?" Captain Asher asked.

"Fine." Theresa moved her massaging from her left knee to her right. "Just growing pains."

"You mean *grown* pains." BB looked at the four crew members, who now ranged in age from their early thirties to their midforties. "You're all so, so old."

"Not as old as you," Arlonus said.

"Huh?"

"Although you do look good for forty-eight hundred years old."

"Huh?" BB scratched his belly. He always scratched his belly when confused or frightened.

"Technically, Arlonus is correct." Dr. Kibbleman, like any teacher or professor, couldn't resist the opportunity to step forward and explain. "You see, this is the year 6789, which makes you the oldest people ever."

Dr. Kibbleman wished he had a pointer and a few charts, or at least some moonchalk and a floating blackboard. "You see, we aged back into our adult bodies as we returned to our time. And as for you—"

"Wonderful," D7, the ship's android, interrupted. She had turned herself on automatically as the *Meatloaf* approached its destination. "Mama Droid's time-displacement patches worked perfectly." She pulled the stamp-sized patch off BB's forehead. "If it weren't for these, you'd be grown-ups like the rest of the crew."

"Thank you." BB gave D7 a hug. "Thank you, thank you, thank you." Being a grown-up was not one of BB's goals. He intended to avoid it as long as possible.

"Everyone take your places, please." Captain Asher had returned to the driver's seat. "We're home." Within moments the *Meatloaf* had landed.

In the storage compartment, two heads of greasy hair, two beefy brows and two pairs of beady little eyes appeared briefly over a row of waste barrels and toxic contaminant containers. Despite the fact that they were stowaways, Bertha and Beula Butterman felt right at home on the *Meatloaf.* Two of the barrels had small cracks, which made the compartment smell much like Beula's bedroom . . . *after* a good cleaning. They peeked out of the storage-compartment window, hoping to see the crew in the main cabin.

Bertha smirked a satisfied smirk. "See." She poked her sister in the ribs, getting her hand momentarily caught in the folds of Beula's flab. "I told you they were time travelers."

"You said they were space monsters."

"You are so picky," Bertha snarled.

"I used to be," Beula admitted. "But remember how Mom taped all my fingers together to make me stop?"

Bertha shuddered. That had been an ugly scene at the emergency room. It had taken the doctors two hours to remove Beula's entire left hand from her right nostril.

Just then Captain Asher walked by the storage-room window.

"Get down, you dinglehead." Bertha pulled Beula down by the time-displacement patch on her chin.

The sisters had discovered a box of D7's time-displacement patches after sneaking onto the *Meatloaf*. They had followed the directions on the box, were unaffected by the time travel and remained their grown-up selves.

As Bertha pulled, the patch tore from her sister's face like a tight bandage. Beula screamed in agony. She had accidentally placed the patch over her prized mole, and when it was yanked off, it pulled out the three white and three black mole hairs of which she was so proud.

Bertha tried to hide her smile. She had always been jealous of those hairs.

In the starship's main compartment, D7 would have loved to hear that her patches worked on hairy as well as nonhairy parts of the body. However, she was too busy pushing the right buttons to open the door, and nobody heard Beula's scream because of the cheers of the crowd.

Two

The crowd numbered in the hundreds of thousands. Cheering people stretched out halfway to the artificially colored horizon. As soon as D7 popped open the hatch, the hero's welcome began.

Captain Asher walked into the hatchway and held a thirty-two-ounce bottle of ketchup over her head. The crowd went from crazy to berserk. She slowly turned the bottle around to show the recipe on the back. Berserk was instantly abandoned in favor of bonkers.

One look at the sea of screaming faces scared BB into ditching his desire to experience all the fast food that the sixty-eighth century had to offer. Ellie suggested a possible change in plans. "You know, maybe you should take us home now. I think my mom's calling."

"Nonsense," Dr. Kibbleman said. "Come on.

Let's enjoy the moment." Dr. K. pushed the students out of the *Meatloaf* and into the crowd.

BB and his friends expected to be instantly crushed by the roaring horde of wildly partying people. They fell forward into the celebration with their arms covering their faces. But instead of running into a wall of wackos, they tripped over each other and fell to the ground. When they looked up, the crowd was gone. The enormous concrete lot in which the *Meatloaf* had landed was empty.

The four shocked students looked back at the crew members, who were nonchalantly unloading their luggage and arguing over who should be elected the next vice-mayor of Mars.

"What happened to all the people?" BB asked, climbing slowly to his feet.

"Yeah, where'd they go?" Perry seconded the question.

"What people?" Arlonus dropped a duffel bag, which thanks to its antigravity strap, floated slowly down before coming to a hover an inch or two above the cement.

"Try, like the gagillion people who were just here?" Ellie put her hands on her hips and rolled her eyes.

The crew looked quite confused until D7 whispered something into Dr. Kibbleman's ear.

"Oh," Dr. K. said, as if he had come to a sudden understanding of a great mystery. "Those people weren't people."

"Then what were they?" Ellie asked.

"VR2245 hologram units," Captain Asher answered while guiding two large, floating trunks out of the *Meatloaf.*

"They weren't real?" Joyce asked. "Just holograms?"

"Not *just* holograms." Dr. K. happily welcomed yet another opportunity to explain. "Everyone in this century has a VR2245 unit. What it does is actually let you see, touch, feel and otherwise experience major historical events without ever leaving home. It's really quite a good idea. Everyone can be everywhere at once. I'll give you some material to study and some work screens to go over."

As Dr. K. walked back into the *Meatloaf,* Ellie turned to BB. "Homework?"

BB grimaced. "You know, he was much cooler when he was twelve."

Ellie nodded. "Isn't everyone?"

Before BB could answer with a resounding *yes,* D7 brought down the last of the crew's carry-ons.

"All right, all," Captain Asher said, pulling a parking lot ticket stub from her pants pocket. "We have to get to my starbus, get home and get ready for tonight's victory banquet."

"Banquet is good." BB felt his stomach start to rumble and ready itself for a BB food binge.

Captain Asher and the crew had rocketpooled to the launching pad for the mission to save fuel. The captain had dropped the crew off to check their bags before finding a parking place.

"Where'd you park?" Arlonus asked.

"The short-term planet." Captain Asher smiled. "I knew we wouldn't be gone long."

"Only five thousand years," Ellie joked.

A moment later a yellow, driverless space shuttle bus pulled up. A beam of turquoise light flew from the bus and engulfed the luggage, which instantly disappeared. "Come on," Captain Asher said. "Time's a-wasting."

The students and crew piled onto the shuttle, leaving D7 alone with the *Meatloaf*.

"Aren't you coming with us?" BB asked.

"I'll see you all later." D7 reached up to close the shuttle door. "I have a lot of straightening up to do. You know what they say, an android's work is never done."

D7 didn't know it at the time, but her busy day had just begun.

While every member of the crew, and all the students, were outside the starship, the *Meatloaf* was far from empty. The two Butterman sisters had left the storage closet and were exploring the spacecraft.

"What does this thing do?"

Before Bertha could stop her sister, Beula pulled a long handle with a red ball on the end. She hadn't bothered to read the words printed on the ball: DANGER. ZERO GRAVITY INDUCER. DO NOT PULL.

Beula pulled . . . *twice* . . . with both hands. She pulled so hard that the handle broke off, sending her flying through the air, across the cabin of the *Meatloaf*. In this case, what went up didn't come down. As soon as the handle snapped, Beula and Bertha's lifelong weight problems vanished. In fact they became weightless and started floating around the starship like two screaming blimps in a bottle.

Slowly, everything that wasn't nailed, bolted, fastened or force-fielded in place floated up to join the flying Buttermans. Last night's dinner dishes drifted by, as did the morning's coffee.

Bertha pushed her way through knives, forks, spoons, sunglasses, sonic toothbrushes and floating synthoflowers. She grabbed Beula by the collar and spun her around in the air.

"Wheeeeeeee!" Beula screamed.

"Shut uuuuuuuuup!" Bertha growled. "Dooooooooooo something, doughnut-hole."

"What do you want—" Beula spit out some old Kleenexes that had left the trash can and floated into her mouth. "What do you want me to do?"

"Anything." Bertha dodged a couple of real-life flying saucers. "Do anything."

"Should I push this button?"

"Yes, anything," Bertha said before looking at the button. When she did look, her tone changed dramatically. "No! Anything but that!"

"What?" Beula said as she picked wax from her ear with her left index finger and pushed the button marked CEILING FAN with her right.

As D7 waved to the departing space shuttle bus, she heard what sounded like a hailstorm erupt from inside the starship. The android sighed a mechanical sigh, knowing that her plans for a nice bubboil bath would have to be put on hold. "Now what?" she moaned while turning and slowly walking toward the suddenly very noisy *Meatloaf.*

Meanwhile, Hurricane Beula was blowing up a storm. As soon as the fan started, Bertha was buffeted from one end of the cabin to the other and back again and again.

In the gravity-free environment, there was no way to stop and nothing to slow her down. Beula attempted to hang on to the fan control dial, but was ripped away when she accidentally turned it from High to Turbo-blow.

Both Buttermans blew around the room in a blur. They were joined by every shred of space junk and loose piece of litter in the *Meatloaf.* They smashed into walls, control panels and furniture. Chunks of whatever they hit would crack off, and join in the spin cycle that wouldn't stop.

Beula slammed into the wall above the door. She was instantly pinned in place by three knives, two forks, several pencils and a pair of titanium scissors. The pointy pieces pierced her clothing and were driven into the wall by the strong wind.

"Hel—" Bertha tried to scream, but the *p*

never made it out of her mouth, which was quickly stuffed with a flying sock, a pair of Arlonus's boxer shorts and a pickle. A Rogarian disposable razor blade did cut through her clothing and end up in her belly button. There it floated in the cavernous darkness, never so much as leaving a scratch on the stretch-mark–covered walls. She spit the clothes from her mouth and swallowed the pickle.

"You . . ." Bertha flew by her sister. ". . . Dip . . . ," she said on her next pass. ". . . Stick!" She completed the insult on the third orbit, which was changed when she attempted to angrily pop her sister in the paunch. The punch missed, and Bertha ended up spinning off like a flabby, furry, 396-pound Frisbee.

"Humans," D7 muttered under her exhaust. "If it isn't one thing it's another." She pushed open the starship door and took a step inside. Instantly her circuits went to red alert, and her emergency anti-antigravity program activated. Her penny-loafer footpads formed an atomic lock with the floor, and every bolt, screw and nut in her body was secured firmly in place.

"Okay," D7 said. "Who left the inducer on?"

The android stood with her hands on her hips, shaking her head in the cyclone of paper, pots and spare starship parts.

Out of D7's visual range, Bertha had managed to wedge herself, upside down, into a new, galaxy-class porta-pot. When she saw the light streaming in from the open door, she stopped screaming. Now, all she could do was hold on tight and hope for the best.

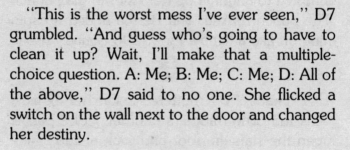

"This is the worst mess I've ever seen," D7 grumbled. "And guess who's going to have to clean it up? Wait, I'll make that a multiple-choice question. A: Me; B: Me; C: Me; D: All of the above," D7 said to no one. She flicked a switch on the wall next to the door and changed her destiny.

Beula Butterman looked straight down at the top of D7's head. When the android hit the gravity restoration switch, her clothes ripped away from the pencils and utensils and she started to fall.

D7 heard a rip, a shrill scream, and the unmistakable approaching odor of onions and old underwear. She looked up just in time to see the monstrous falling mass that was Beula Butterman. It was the last thing D7 would remember seeing for a very long time.

A crashing, bashing, crunching sound filled the *Meatloaf*. It was followed by the noise of several hundred pounds of flab smacking against a metal floor. It was not a pretty sound.

It took a few minutes, but Beula slowly managed to roll off D7 and get to her feet. She looked down at the smashed android, and if she could have, she would have jumped for joy. "Hey, Berth," she called out. "I got the mom."

Instead of the applause she expected, Beula heard Bertha's muffled, gurgling cries for help. When gravity had been restored to the new porta-pot, she had fallen headfirst where no one had gone before.

"Get me out of here." Bertha struggled, but was stuck tight. "And for Flatbush sake, don't flush."

After flushing . . . *twice* . . . and with the

help of an industrial-sized plunger, Beula freed her sister from the toilet bowl with a loud pop. The force released when Bertha broke loose sent both sisters tumbling across the starship floor.

"What part of *don't flush* didn't you understand, potty-brain?" Bertha roared.

"Don't," Beula answered.

Bertha started whapping her sister in the face with her sopping wet hair, and continued to do so until it was almost dry. Then the two sisters looked around the starship, which was a shambles of rubble and fallen debris.

"So this is the sixty-eighth century." Beula dried her face on her sleeves. "What do we do now?"

Suddenly a tiny, mechanical, recorded voice spoke from the wreckage of D7. "Reprogram, please. Reprogram, please. Damaged android. Reprogram, please."

Bertha looked at Beula and smiled.

Three

After everyone was strapped into Captain Asher's Starbus, it was decided that Ellie, BB, Joyce and Perry would be divided up between the three adults who had kids their age. In that way they'd all get a slightly different taste of sixty-eighth-century life. Captain Asher dropped BB and Dr. Kibbleman off first.

"Bianca, I'd like you to meet BB. BB . . . Bianca. Bianca . . . BB," Dr. Kibbleman introduced BB to his twelve-year-old daughter. "BB's from around the turn of the century," Dr. K. said to Bianca. "Almost fifty turns ago."

"Nice to meetcha." BB stuck out his hand.

"What's he doing?" Bianca stepped back and looked at her dad. "Why does he have his arm out like that?"

"It's an ancient greeting," Dr. K. said. "It's called shaking hands."

"Is it friendly?"

"Oh, yes, very."

"Okay." Bianca sounded skeptical, but she stuck her arm straight out in front of her and started wildly shaking her hand in the air.

BB lowered his arm. "I think you have a lot to learn about shaking hands."

"Oh, do I, now?" Bianca walked up to BB and poked him in the belly.

"Ouch!"

"You're . . . you're . . . *real.*"

"You're . . . you're . . . *loony.*" Now it was BB who backed away. He patted what had just been poked.

"I'm sorry." Bianca blushed. "I thought you were one of Dad's history holograms. Last week he brought home Thomas Edison, Pablo Picasso and Zipknockspree of Zelton."

"Zip what?" BB stopped patting.

"Don't ask."

"Okay."

"Hey," Dr. K. said, "I thought the old Zipper gave an interesting dinner talk."

"On the Zeltonian gamma-ray shortage of 5997?" Bianca rolled her eyes. "Fascinating."

"It was educational," Dr. K. stated as he walked out of the room. "You know it doesn't hurt to *learn* something now and again."

Bianca walked over to BB. "Were parents like that back when you were alive?"

"Nah," BB said.

"Really?"

"They were worse." BB hesitated. "I mean . . . they *are* worse."

"Yep." Bianca nodded. "Raising parents isn't easy."

"It never was," BB agreed.

"Anyway." Bianca changed the subject. "Come on, let's go play inside for a while."

"Uh, Bianca," BB said while looking around the room. "I think we're already inside."

Bianca started to laugh. "I think you're the one who has a lot to learn."

She took BB by one hand and led him over to what looked like a control panel with three monitors and rows of little flashing lights. She tightened her grip on his hand. "Hang on." She placed her other hand on a darkened area of the control panel. Instantly she and BB vanished, leaving only their shoes behind them.

Joyce and Perry got out with Arlonus Quick. His twin son and daughter, Kurt and Connie, met them at the door. They barely noticed the visitors. They were too busy arguing over who was responsible for vaporizing a neighbor's window and for the molecular destruction of the new cable-ready mind-a-vision that their dad had bought just before the launch of Project Ketchup.

Arlonus groaned and looked back at Captain Asher for help. For her part, Captain Asher floored her starbus, going from zero to sixty times the sound barrier in 4.3 seconds. "When the Quick kids get going . . . it's time to get out."

A few moments later the bus stopped and hovered in front of Theresa's very high-rise apartment. "See you tonight." Theresa pulled a small black remote-control device from her briefcase. She pushed the third button on the left, which instantly beamed her into her bath, complete with bubbles, bath oil and her favorite book.

While Theresa sighed and settled into the suds, Captain Asher made a downward U-turn, which momentarily had the bus upside down. "You're with me!" Captain Asher said to Ellie while rolling the bus through the air until they were back in their original upright position. "I can't wait for you to meet my son. He's exactly your age." Captain Asher started to laugh.

"What's so funny?" Ellie asked.

"It's weird to think that just a few minutes ago, my son was actually almost seven years older than me."

"Yeah." Ellie watched as two people on spaceboards zoomed by, above the van. " 'Weird' sounds just about right to me."

BB and Bianca were falling, although BB couldn't tell if they were falling up or down. There was absolutely no sound until BB started to scream.

"Don't be a baby," Bianca scolded. "It's just a game."

"I'm not screaming!" BB screamed as they fell. "I'm, uh, cheering! Do you have a problem with that?"

Before Bianca could answer, they both landed softly in the strangest world BB had ever seen. The ground was brown and solid, but BB felt as if he were standing on a cloud. The air was fresher than any he had ever breathed before, and the sky was so deeply blue that it was almost purple. It was sunny, but there was no sun. In fact, there was nothing at all but sky and earth.

"Where are we?" BB asked.

"Anywhere you want to be." Bianca let go of BB's hand and walked a few steps away. "I usually like to start with a little Tylorian Snake Lizard to warm up. You first."

Suddenly BB felt the ground beneath his feet open and himself being dragged down. In less that a blink, only his head remained above the mushy earth. A second later the twin heads of a Tylorian snake lizard pushed up through the ground, about three feet from BB's nose. The one eye on each head flamed orange-red, and barbed horns popped out from the back of its skulls. When it hissed, it showed its rows of razor-sharp teeth, which spun like fan blades and sparkled in the light.

The snake lizard opened its powerful jaws wide; its eyes flared; it rushed directly at BB's face. This time BB didn't pretend to be cheering. He screamed loudly as the heads raced closer. His scream was only muffled when one of the heads bit down over his mouth and the other over his eyes. Then, as their mouths started to close and chew, the heads disappeared, leaving only a laughing Bianca Kibbleman sitting cross-legged in front of BB.

"You lose," she giggled. "Want to play again?"

"Hi," Connie Quick said. "Don't mind my brother, Kurt, a.k.a. Jerkbutt."

"Nice to meet you," Kurt said to Perry and Joyce as if he hadn't heard a word. "And don't mind my sister, Connie, a.k.a. Fart-monkey."

The twins looked at each other like world-champion wrestlers about to declare war.

"No name-calling." Arlonus stepped between them. "And no fighting."

"Us? Fight?" Connie hugged her dad and secretly stuck her tongue out at her brother. In turn, her brother made some sort of hand gesture that Joyce and Perry didn't understand but that made Connie's face turn beet red with anger.

"Now," Arlonus said, "where's Mom? I want her to meet our five-thousand-year-old guests."

"Five thousand years old?" Kurt said. "Wow, what grade are you in?"

"Sixth," Joyce answered.

"Boy, talk about being held back."

"They're not really five thousand." Connie smiled at what she thought was her brother's stupidity. "They're just—"

"It was a joke." Kurt chopped each word.

"Oh." Connie frowned. "I knew that."

"Let's rewind and push Play again, shall we?" Arlonus said. "Where's Mom?"

"After Kurt vaporized the window—"

"*Connie* vaporized the window—" Kurt interrupted.

Connie continued. "Mom said she had a lot of errands to do—on Mars."

Just then a very angry neighbor called out through what used to be a window. He strongly requested an immediate meeting with Arlonus.

"We need to talk," Arlonus said to Kurt and Connie as he reached for his wallet and headed toward the neighbor's.

"So, what now?" Perry asked.

Connie and Kurt watched their dad step on the neighbor's welcome-mat transporter. He was instantly beamed inside.

"Whatever we do," Kurt said, "I think we better hurry, and I think it better be far away."

"How about Disney World?" Connie suggested.

"In Florida?" Joyce asked.

"What's a Florida?" Kurt asked Perry while Connie answered Joyce's question.

"No. I mean Disney *World*."

"Where's that?"

Connie pointed straight up. "You just go fifteen million light-years and turn left."

"Why do they call you Pokey?"

Captain Asher's son seemed somewhat embarrassed by Ellie's question. "I was the slowest flyer in kindergarten," he answered. "My friend Bianca started calling me that, and it just sorta stuck."

"What's your real name?"

"Aloysius Poindexter Asher the third."

"Pleased to meet you, . . . Pokey." Ellie smiled. "Where do you want to go?"

Captain Asher had dropped Ellie off at her home on the starbase before going off to turn in the ketchup recipes and file her report on the mission. She had asked Pokey to show their guest around the sixty-eighth century.

"Can Ellie use your bike?" Pokey had asked.

"As long as you both remember to wear your helmets," Captain Asher answered as she stepped onto a transporter pad, waved goodbye and vanished.

"You up for a bike tour?" Pokey turned to Ellie.

"Sure," Ellie said. "Sounds like fun."

"I hope you don't mind riding Mom's old ten-speed."

"My mom has an old ten-speed too." Ellie laughed. "Antique city."

Pokey laughed as well. "Maybe they both shopped at the same flea market."

Captain Asher's bike looked like a red version of Ellie's mom's Blue Bomber. Ellie hopped on and was about to start pedaling when a somewhat frantic Pokey jumped in front of her and blocked her path. "Wait, you forgot your helmet." He handed Ellie what looked like an ordinary black bike helmet. "Never ride without one of these."

"Cool it," Ellie said. "I was just going to ride around right here while you got your bike."

"That's so dangerous," Pokey said. "Remember, most accidents happen within thirty million miles of home." Pokey paused. ". . . And why do you want me to lower the temperature of your helmet? Is it too warm?"

"Never mind," Ellie said. *Dorkus-orelius,* she thought.

Pokey just shook his head, put on his helmet and walked over toward his bike. "Now wait, and follow me. These bikes, especially the older ones, can be a bit tricky."

"Oh, yeah . . . right." Ellie sighed.

"What's right?"

Ellie didn't answer the question. She never liked to follow anyone. She particularly didn't like being told to follow someone. She also considered herself an expert behind the handlebars and was insulted by Pokey's telling her to be careful. *Tricky, my toejam,* she thought, and started to pedal.

Instantly Ellie wished that, in this particular instance, she had followed Pokey's advice. She immediately realized that the trick was on her.

As soon as Ellie pushed down on the pedals, the bike started to rise. By the third revolution of the wheels, she was at least a hundred feet in the air. The ordinary helmet transformed itself into a clear, glasslike bowl that surrounded her head. All sorts of weather readings, traffic-pattern diagrams, star charts and an occasional advertisement floated by in front of her eyes.

Ellie tried squeezing the hand brakes, but when she did, the bike nose-dived straight for the ground. Ellie let go, pedaled harder and rose higher. When she reached five hundred feet, a clear, solid-looking bubble, much like the helmet, encased the entire bike. More figures, equations and a reminder to eat at Jupiter Joe's flashed in the air before Ellie's startled eyes. Still, she kept pedaling harder and rising higher.

Suddenly Pokey, in helmet and bubble-enclosed bike, pulled alongside her. "Put it on autopedal," he called out.

"What?"

"Autopedal." Pokey pushed his hand through his bubble and into Ellie's. It looked as if he were moving it through clear Jell-O. Ellie watched as he switched the gearshift on the left of the handlebar. The words AUTOPEDAL ACTIVATED moved from left to right in front of her face.

"*Stop pedaling,*" Pokey yelled.

"I'll crash," Ellie called back.

"Nuh-uh."

"Uh-huh!"

"Look." Pokey switched the left shifter on his own handlebar and lifted his feet off his pedals. "See?"

Ellie envisioned herself splattered across the sixty-eighth-century countryside, but she slowly lifted her feet anyway. The pedals kept turning, and the bike's path leveled off.

"Now tell your bike to land," Pokey said.

Ellie looked down. She could see several shining silver cities and what appeared to be an ocean on the horizon. She didn't ask any questions. "Land." She looked down again. "Please."

The next instant Ellie and her bike were back on solid ground. The bike helmet was once again an ordinary black bike helmet, and the bicycle bubble had burst.

Pokey skidded to a stop in the dirt next to her. "Are you okay? I knew I should have put on some training rockets."

"I thought you said this was a ten-speed." Ellie tried to slow her breathing and her heartbeat.

"It is," Pokey said. "It can't go more than ten times the speed of light."

"No wonder I had a problem." Ellie felt her stomach start to return to something resembling normal. "It's too slow."

Four

"**Man, it was so cool.** I ended up eating both heads and the tail." BB told everyone about Bianca's dream-simulation chamber, and how he had become a master at Tylorian Snake Lizard.

"And it only took him one hundred thirty-seven tries," Bianca laughed.

"You should see the Moons of Mickey," Joyce said happily.

"Yeah," Perry jumped in. "And when they call a ride Space Mountain, they mean *space mountain*."

Perry and Joyce described their trip as everyone waited for the celebration banquet to begin. They had all been flown to the banquet hall in a stretch limosaucer and directed to a small room behind the stage. Captain Asher and crew were going to be awarded the Golden Meatloaf of

Valor for bringing home the ketchup. Ellie, BB, Perry and Joyce were the special guests of honor and were scheduled to each receive the Silver Meatball for assisting in the mission.

"So . . ." BB turned to Ellie, who was strangely silent. "What did you do today?"

Ellie gave Pokey a shut-up-or-you're-onion-dip look and said, "Not much. We just went for a little bike ride."

"Yeah," Pokey said with a grin. "Ellie was flying all over the place."

"She always was a showoff," BB said as two women in space cadet uniforms entered the room. They signaled everyone that it was time for them to make their grand entrance and receive a hero's welcome.

When they walked into the hall, several thousand adults stood up and cheered. Perry and Joyce were a little frightened, while Ellie just waved and BB blew kisses to the crowd. They all walked up onto a stage, which held a pure-white table. The captain and crew of the *Meatloaf* were already in their places, and joined in the applause.

The five-thousand-year-old sixth-graders, remembering their experiences on the starship, didn't hesitate to sit down on the clear blobby things that were lined up by the table. As expected, as soon as they sat down, the blobs formed into chairs around them, each perfectly molded and heated to fit its particular sitter.

"I really gotta get one of these for home." BB shifted his weight from one hip to the other, feeling the chair compensate for the movement almost before it happened. He moved back and forth, up and down and around and around, but the seat always seemed to be a half move ahead of BB's behind.

"Ahhhhhh." BB took a deep breath and settled in. "So, when do we eat? I feel as if I haven't had a bite in centuries."

"Right after the speeches," Bianca said.

From the look on her new friend's face, Bianca could tell that he didn't like her answer one bit. "Don't worry, the speeches will be short, and the food here is always great. It'll be worth the wait."

"Can I at least get something to drink?"

"Sure," Pokey said. "What do you want to drink?"

"A pizza."

Ellie poked BB in the ribs. "Come on, be serious."

"Okay, okay," BB said bitterly. He had been serious about the pizza. "What do you have to drink?"

"Anything you want," Bianca said. "Just ask."

BB looked around. There wasn't a waiter in sight. "Ask whom?"

"The table, silly. Watch." Bianca put her hand out on the table as if she were already holding a glass. "Synth-Aid, please. Lemon."

Instantly her once-empty hand now held a tall, frothy glass of what appeared to be lemonade.

"I love this century." BB held out his hand. "Dr Pepper, please." He smiled. "Stat." BB turned to Bianca, who had a confused look on her face. He felt something in his hand. When he squeezed, the "something" squeezed back.

"Hey!" BB jumped up out of his chair and away from the man who had been holding his hand while he checked his pulse. "Who are you?"

"Doctor Pepper," the man said. "Dr. Peter Pepper. What seems to be the problem?"

"I don't need a doctor, I need a drink," BB said loudly.

"Then why didn't you ask for one instead of calling me?"

"I didn't call you. I asked for Dr Pepper."

"I'm here, what seems to be the problem?"

"I don't need a doctor!"

35

"Excuse me, Doctor. I'm so sorry." Bianca stepped in. "Wrong number."

The doctor sighed, gave BB a dirty look and vanished.

"Be more careful about what you order," Bianca said. "No more pranking."

BB just shook his head and held out his hand. "Sprite, please."

A tiny fairy appeared. Its fluttering wings tickled BB's hand.

"*Gatorade!*" BB screamed. The fairy was immediately replaced by a snapping baby alligator.

BB flipped the gator into the air. It vanished as soon as it left his hand. He noticed that Ellie, Perry and Joyce were in near hysterics, while Bianca, Pokey and the Quick twins were looking at him as if he were a bit on the odd side of totally wacked.

BB moaned, settled back into his seat and said, "Oh, okay. Just give me Hi-C, any flavor." A high-frequency tone filled the hall. Everyone turned and looked at BB. "The drink, not the note." BB banged his head on the table three times. "Hi-C, Hi-C, Hi-C." Every time he placed his order, the tone sounded.

Bianca was getting a bit nervous with all the

adults staring at them. "Stop playing and ask for a drink. Everyone's looking."

Ellie looked at BB, who was about to bang again. She grabbed his hair as his head started to drop, and yanked back.

"*Ow!*" BB shouted.

"Stop it," Ellie ordered. "You're giving our century a bad name."

"It's not my fault." BB looked angrily at Ellie. "I'd like to see you order something to drink."

Ellie put her right hand out on the table and pointed at Bianca with her left. "I'll have what she's having."

A glass matching Bianca's appeared in Ellie's hand, and BB started to cry.

Bertha and Beula Butterman started to laugh. They hid behind what appeared to be a solid portable wall, off to one side of the banquet hall.

"Watch this one," Bertha snorted as she stuck her nose up to, against and then through the force field, which had been made to look like a partition.

The Butterman sisters were having a great time spying and sticking body parts through the force field, until Beula swung a meaty hip through and accidentally sent a man somersaulting across the hall. While staying hidden behind the force field, they quickly ran to the front of the room and crammed themselves under the stage, where all the guests of honor were finally being served the meal they had been waiting for.

"What's this stuff?" BB carefully lifted the green-and-yellow square that a waiter had placed on his plate. He turned it over twice before putting it back down next to the red triangle, blue circle, orange oval and multicolored hexagon with three white marbles attached to one side.

"The square is your synthoveggies," Bianca answered BB's question.

"And the red triangle?" Ellie asked.

"Synthochicken. I think it might be extra crispy." Bianca went on to explain that the blue circle was synthosoup, the orange oval synthotatoes, and the multi-colored hexagon was synthosalad, with synthoranch dressing on the side.

"Go on," Pokey said while cutting the corner of his red triangle. "Eat up. It's delicious."

While everyone carefully cut or nibbled around the edges, BB took matters into his own hands. He picked up all five forms and smushed them into one small ball, which he happily tossed into his mouth. After the first bite there was no mistaking the flavor that filled BB's mouth. The ball tasted like a corn-and-green-bean, chicken-extra-crispy, pea-soup, mashed-potato, tossed-salad rice cake—with a little ranch on the side.

"Okay." BB swallowed. "So when do we *really* eat?"

"You just did," Connie said as she carefully munched a bit of synthotato. "This is dinner."

"Yeah?" BB's stomach rumbled a protest that could be heard two tables away. "Then what's for dessert?"

When no one said a word, BB repeated his plea. "Maybe you didn't hear me. I said, what's for dessert?"

Again there was absolutely no response, just blank stares.

"I don't think they know what you're talking about," Ellie whispered into BB's ear.

BB nodded. "You know," he said. "Something sweet after a meal."

"Oh." Pokey poked Kurt to get his attention.

Kurt poked his sister for fun. "He means nutritional supplement six." Pokey signaled for a waiter. "Can we see your nutritional-supplement-six tray, please?"

A moment later the waiter glided a floating tray up to the front table. It was filled with many colored forms and shapes, each on its own small plate.

"Here's my favorite." Pokey picked up a plate containing a purple diamond-shaped thing.

"What is it?" BB asked.

"It's synthofat-free, sugar-free, yogurtlike food substitute Zilon 26. I guess you'd call it . . . oh, what was that word again?"

"Dessert?" BB offered.

"Yes, dessert." Pokey smiled. "Here's your dessert." He handed BB a plate.

BB looked down at what could have passed for a purple Colorform. "I don't think this is exactly what I had in mind."

"Dessert!" Beula Butterman tried to stand up. Unfortunately for her, the area under the stage offered barely enough scrunching room, much less enough space to come to full attention. When she tried to rise, she slammed into the floorboards, making the entire stage tremble and shake.

Captain Asher picked up her communicator and called Environmental Control to report a possible unscheduled earthquake.

To BB, the synthodessert, like the other food, tasted like stale rice cakes, except this time there might have been a vague, hidden hint of something that might have once been frosting.

"How do you like it?" Bianca asked.

BB wanted to be polite. The best he could do was: "It's so gross!" BB tried to wipe the crumbs of the catastrophic taste test off his tongue.

"Is *gross* good?" Kurt asked.

"I don't think so," Connie said as she watched BB spit bits of Zilon 26 into his napkin.

"Don't you have any real dessert?" BB asked while secretly dropping his napkin under the table.

"Like what?" Pokey asked.

"Like this." BB pulled out the three emergency candy bars he always carried with him. "I don't leave home without 'em." He smiled. He tore open the wrapper.

A faint, strange aroma filled the banquet hall.

It was like nothing anyone had ever experienced before. The scent was dizzying . . . beautiful . . . delicious.

BB took a bite of the candy bar. As soon as he did, the aroma doubled, tripled and quadrupled in intensity. Every real mouth in the room started to water. Those attending via hologram immediately left their homes and headed for the banquet hall as soon as their smell-a-vision units kicked in.

Everyone was drawn to the stage by this all-powerful, practically irresistible scent. It came from the ancient one called BB. More specifically, it came from what he held in his hand.

BB thought he'd done something horribly wrong. Everyone was moving toward him. In a second he was surrounded by shocked, startled faces. People and holograms alike had wild looks in their eyes and were reaching out with straining, clutching fingers.

BB tried to back up but ran into the real people who had closed in behind him. He didn't know what he'd done, or what to do.

"I—I'm sorry about the rice cakes," he stammered. "I'll pick up the napkin. I promise."

BB gestured with the candy bar toward the table. It passed beneath the noses of several people, causing them to faint from pure plea-sure.

A woman in a military uniform with lots of stars, bars and ribbons pointed at BB's hand. "What . . . What *is* that?"

"Oh, *this*?" BB held up the candy bar. "It's just chocolate."

"Choc-o-late?"

"Chocolate," BB answered. "Want a bite?"

"Choc-o-late," the woman said. She turned to the crowd. "Choc-o-late. Choc-o-late. Choc-o-late."

Everyone started to chant "Choc-o-late . . . choc-o-late . . . choc-o-late . . ."

BB turned to Ellie, who couldn't believe her eyes or ears. "I'll tell you one thing," BB said. "These are my kind of people."

"Choc-o-late . . . choc-o-late . . . choc-o-late . . ."

BB handed out small pieces of the candy until all three bars were gone. Once the last magnifi-cent morsel was munched, the chant changed from   "Choc-o-late . . . choc-o-late . . . choc-o-late . . ." to "More . . . more . . . more . . ."

Five

Bertha Butterman had a devilish grin on her face and a communicator in her hand. "B7," she said into the device, "beam us home."

"Check, sister," a semimechanical voice responded. "Stand by."

It took a moment for the equipment to adjust to their mass, but within seconds the Buttermans disappeared from their hiding place and reappeared in the *Meatloaf*.

The cries for more were deafening and insistent. BB walked up to a blue crystal podium. He raised his hands for quiet, but this crowd would simply not be silenced.

BB looked at Captain Asher for help. She

nodded and pulled out her phaser. She set the weapon on delayed overload and placed it on the table. The high, shrieking sound of a phaser gone critical finally got the crowd's attention.

"Danger . . . Danger. . . . Phaser explosion in thirty seconds." The warning sounded throughout the hall.

"D7," Captain Asher said calmly into her communicator. "Please lock onto phaser R42 and beam it to deep space."

Captain Asher had used this trick to wake up her troops on several occasions. It always worked. She looked at the phaser, confidently expecting it to dematerialize. It didn't. Instead, the shrieking got louder, and Captain Asher's confidence began to fade.

"Uh, D7? I do suggest you hurry," she called into her communicator.

The shrieking reached ear-splitting proportions and the phaser started to glow blue, then green, then yellow, then red. People began to scream and run.

"D7? D7!" Captain Asher shouted.

The phaser started to shake, rattle and roll around the table. It was starting to lose form, which meant the explosion was seconds away.

Captain Asher turned a dial on her communicator to Military Priority Channel 1. "Emergency! Emergency! Star Command Control. Emergency beam-out. Communicator Coordinates: B-1701. Authorization: Meatloaf Command Ketchup Ketchup Bingo Max!"

Captain Asher dove for the table and put her communicator on the now shimmering, smoking phaser. As she turned to leap away, a purple beam covered the weapon and the table. Both vanished.

Not half of a split second passed before a loud explosion rocked the entire hall, knocking dozens of people to the floor and causing several holographic images to lose vertical control.

"Wow. That was close." Bianca breathed a breath that a moment earlier she hadn't been sure she'd be taking.

"I'll say," Kurt said. "I bet that thing wasn't two light-years away."

"More like one," Connie corrected.

"What happened to D7?" Pokey asked his mom.

Captain Asher felt her fingers burning. She looked at her hand and realized that she hadn't gotten away from the table quite fast enough. The fingernails on her right hand, the ones that had held the communicator, were substantially shorter than those on her left. The transporter beam had given her the closest manicure of her life. She'd missed being transported with the phaser by less than a centimeter.

"D7's never failed before." Pokey shook his head. "What could have gone wrong?"

"Trust me." Captain Asher blew on her tingling, stinging fingers. "I fully intend to find out."

About thirty seconds earlier Captain Asher's request to beam out an overloading phaser had been received in the *Meatloaf*.

"What does that mean, B7?" Beula asked the android she and her sister had so recently reprogrammed. They had imprinted on D7's circuits all the traits that made them the Buttermans. The android now thought she was their long-lost sister, B7.

"It means," B7 answered, "that either I transport that phaser to deep space or . . ."

B7 paused. The Butterman sisters moved in closer and closer to hear, until—*"Kabloo-weeeeeeey!"* B7 shouted, sending Bertha and Beula tumbling onto their backsides.

"You mean if you don't do like she says"—Bertha paused—*"Baboommmmmmm-boooozle?"*

"Yes," B7 said. "So, what should I do?"

After about two seconds of careful consideration, Bertha said, "How's about making lunch?"

Bertha, Beula and B7 giggled mean little giggles of glee, and went about the business of preparing the *Meatloaf* for flight.

Back at the banquet hall, things quickly returned to normal, and the focus of everyone was again squarely directed on the sweetest subject of all . . . chocolate. BB was back behind the podium, and as honorary Doctor of Chocolate, he was prepared to answer any and all questions, queries and concerns.

"Those three bars you had. Was that all the chocolate that exists?" a woman asked.

BB smiled and looked around the room. Every eye in the place was on him. A hushed silence fell over the crowd. BB knew they were all waiting for him to speak. *This is so cool,* BB thought as he said, "People . . . you ain't ate nothing yet."

"There's more?" a holographic image of a man in a yellow suit asked.

"Don't get me started." BB began naming

every chocolate bar and dessert he knew, which was pretty much every chocolate bar and dessert that existed. He went from chocolate kisses to chocolate cream pie, from hot fudge to devil's food cake, and from Goobers to every type of gloppy goody he could think of.

The people in the room didn't know a thing BB was talking about, but that didn't matter. It was clear from the list of strange words that sprang from BB's lips that the past did indeed contain more chocolate . . . and plenty of it.

"Oh, poodle-piddle," Beula complained while looking at a monitor that showed the banquet hall. "It didn't blow up," she whined. "Can't anything ever go right?"

"Don't worry, it's not your fault," Bertha comforted her sister. "Sometimes accidents just don't happen."

"You're so smart," Beula said. "If I hadn't gotten the looks in the family I wouldn't have anything." Beula felt her mole to see if the hairs had started to grow back.

Bertha changed the subject. "Shut up and strap in," she said as she rolled into her seat. "It's time to fly."

The starship seat tried to mold around her mighty form, but the best it could do was flatten out like a blanket.

"What are we going to do?" Beula sat down. Her chair disappeared completely.

"We're going to be rich, rich, richer than rich."

"What do you mean?"

Before Bertha could answer, the newest Butterman, B7, asked, "Where to, sis?"

The starship had about a loaf and a half of fuel left—just enough to get to where Bertha wanted to go. "Home." Bertha stuck a time-displacement patch to her forearm and another to Beula's nose. "And step on it."

A few minutes later Captain Asher was about to put her foot down, but Pokey wouldn't give her the chance. "Come on, M-o-o-o-o-o-m. You have to let us go," Pokey pleaded. "You just have to. You're always saying I should take more responsibility. I have to grow up, be an adult. Well, this is your chance to practice what you've preached and give me a chance to be responsible. Come on, M-o-o-o-o-o-o-m."

"No." Captain Asher tried standing her ground. "It's too dangerous."

"Not with the time-displacement patches D7 invented."

"Who told you about those?" Captain Asher hated news leaks.

Ellie excused herself to use the bathroom.

"You know he's right," Bianca said. "We're all space-qualified and cosmos-certified to fly a ketchup-class starship."

"To Neptune or the North Star, of course you're qualified," Captain Asher said. "But this is someplace you've never been."

"*They've* been there." Kurt pointed to BB, Perry and Joyce.

"They've lived there," Connie added.

"We'd be happy to give them the grand tour." BB watched Captain Asher's eyes narrow and her nostrils flare. "Or maybe not," he quickly added, and started investigating his shoes.

Captain Asher couldn't think of anything to say that would make sense. She knew that, logically, Pokey and his friends were fully capable of doing the job. She just didn't want to admit that they were growing up.

The banquet had ended with a voice vote in favor of sending someone back in time once again. Everyone wanted to taste every dessert BB had mentioned. The mission would be called Project Chocolate. Captain Asher reported that the *Meatloaf* still had about a loaf and a half in its tank, so it again became the designated starship. The problem was that the starship crew and captain were tied up with business, experiments and military maneuvers for at least a week. However, no one in the banquet hall was willing to wait for even a minute for more tasty chocolate treats.

"Plus, D7 will be with us," Pokey said. "I'm sure that the phaser thing has a logical explanation."

After another ten minutes of nagging, pleading, begging and promising to fly straight back in time, Captain Asher sighed and tossed Pokey the spare starship keys. "Only if D7 checks out," she said. "And no hotrocketing."

"Love ya, Mom." Pokey gave his mom a big hug and kiss.

"Please, Pokey," she said. "Not in front of the troops."

As they walked out the door, they ran into Dr. Kibbleman, who materialized in their path. He had beamed home briefly to check on a particularly tricky experiment. "Where are you off to?" he asked Bianca.

"Don't worry, Dad," she answered. "We'll be right back. We're just going to pick up some dessert."

ix

"Plan B!" Bertha shouted.
"We got a plan B?" Beula asked.
"Yes."
More phaser blasts filled the air.
"It's a good thing we do."
Bertha and Beula had recently gathered all the Butterman cousins, from Brenda to Babs, to battle what they thought were aliens and, more importantly, to consume the meatloaves. They had advanced on the starship just after the crew and their sixth-grade assistants had filled the vessel with ketchup-rich meatloaves and were about to escape with the recipe for the precious tomato-based fuel. The Buttermans would have none of this. No one left the planet with food that the Buttermans themselves could be eating.

When the Butterman brigade had reached the starship, the *Meatloaf* crew opened fire to scatter the attackers and beam them to Brazil, Budapest, Burma and Buffalo. As the phaser bursts continued, Bertha had pulled Beula away by the mole hairs. "Come on. Hurry, while they're not looking."

In the thick smoke and utter confusion of the moment, Bertha and Beula had slipped away from the group and headed for the *Meatloaf*. They had immediately run directly into . . . themselves.

The Buttermans had arrived just in time to stop themselves from wrecking their own plans. The Bertha and Beula from that morning were determined to stop the *Meatloaf* from taking off. The Buttermans who had just gotten back from the sixty-eighth century were just as determined to let the launch proceed on schedule.

Bertha and Beula looked directly at Bertha and Beula. "Who are you?" Bertha-past snarled.

"We're you," Bertha-future snarled back.

The Buttermans-past weren't buying it. Sure, they found the impostors quite beautiful, ravishing in fact. They also wore the exact same stained black dresses. But this had to be some alien trick. They confirmed this fact in their own minds when they spotted something that they were convinced gave the impostors away.

They stared at it, glared at it and growled as a new round of phaser fire shot overhead. They both looked directly at the same spot on Beula-future's chin.

Beula-past proudly twirled her three white and three black mole hairs with her finger. "You're us, are you?" she hissed, and narrowed her beady little eyes. "Then how come I can do this?" She gave an extra twirl that made the mole hairs curl. "And you can't? Huh, baldy?"

Beula-future's face turned red with rage. She pointed to the Bertha next to her. "She pulled them out . . . on purpose." Beula pointed to the Bertha in front of her. "She *will* pull them out . . . on purpose."

Beula-past looked angrily at her sister. "You always were so jealous of my looks." She stepped forward and stood next to herself. Beula-past hugged Beula-future. "I'm so sorry for me," she sobbed.

Soon both Beulas were hugging, sobbing and drooling uncontrollably. Each wiped her nose on the other's shoulder.

"Okay," Bertha-past said. "Now I believe you. They're both Beulas, all right. So that means . . ." She held out her hand to her duplicate. "Pleased to meet me, Bertha."

Two phaser blasts scorched the earth between the Berthas and the Beulas. Bertha-future decided to get right to the point. "They ain't aliens," she said while pointing toward the starship. "They're future people. You got to hitch a ride with them so that you can become us."

Bertha-future jiggled her own jowls and continued. "You have to go into the future, and you have to do it now."

"But I didn't pack," Beula-past whined.

The Berthas looked at her with can-you-say-anything-more-stupid expressions on their faces.

Beula-past coughed. "Sorry, do continue."

Bertha-future started to explain ketchup-based time travel when their time ran out. The phaser fire stopped. Bertha, Bertha, Beula and Beula looked at their cousins, who were lumbering off in every direction. First Babs vanished, then Bruno, then Brenda.

Bertha-future went nose-to-nose with Bertha-past. At the smell of her own buffalo morning breath, both Berthas backed up a bit. "Listen," Bertha-future said. "There's no time to explain. Just go along for the ride until you become us, okay?'' She reached into her pocket and pulled out—an old slice of pizza.

"Beula!" she snapped. "How many times do I have to tell you not to store your snacks on me?"

Bertha tossed the slice into the air. Both Beulas grabbed it and started a tug-of-pizza. "Mine!" they both yelled. "I put it in there."

Bertha-past reached into her pocket and felt the slice of pizza, double anchovies. She silently vowed to eat it on the trip to the future. She knew that she had kept that vow when the slice that Beula and Beula were fighting over suddenly vanished.

Meanwhile, Bertha-future reached deeper into her pocket and pulled out a slightly cheesy-smelling communicator. "B7," she said into the device. "Meatloaf special. Four. To go."

Bertha and Beula and Beula and Bertha disappeared and instantly found themselves inside two identical Starships *Meatloaf.* Bertha- and Beula-future's space vessel had just recently arrived; Bertha- and Beula-past's was scheduled for immediate departure.

Meanwhile, back in the year 6789, people were dancing in the streets. Those with antigravity tap shoes were dancing above the streets. Everyone loved the idea of sending the *Meatloaf* back for chocolate—lots of chocolate—and it seemed as though the whole world was escorting the new starship crew to the launching area for takeoff.

As one set of Buttermans prepared for an adventure into the unknown, the other set put its plan into action. Beula-future went to a nearby diner and ordered fifteen meatloaf dinners to go. "Double ketchup. Make it snappy."

Bertha-future stayed back in the *Meatloaf* to give B7 her flying orders. "We need a day or two here. Go back to the future. Don't let anyone, particularly that pack of preteen punks, know that you're not the lovable *D7* they think you are."

"But I would have to be sneaky and lie like a Butterman," B7 said.

"Exactly."

B7 and Bertha gave each other the Butterman spit-growl-belch salute just as Beula walked in with eight orders of meatloaf. When Bertha looked at her suspiciously, Beula put up a vigorous defense. "What? That's all they had! I swear it!" As she protested, tiny bits and pieces of meatloaf flew from her mouth. "Hey!" Beula exclaimed. "How did *they* get in there?"

When the sixty-eighth-century crowd arrived at the launching area, the *Meatloaf* appeared unchanged. With the cheering throng behind them, the young crew and Captain Asher walked on board. They were greeted by the smiling android they all knew as D7.

While Pokey, Bianca, Kurt and Connie took up flight positions and BB, Ellie, Joyce and Perry settled into the passenger seats, Captain Asher had a few questions for her mechanical friend. Questions like "Why didn't you beam the overloading phaser out of the banquet hall as ordered?"

D7 looked confused. Then she snapped her fingers. "That must have been when I had my communicator off the hook. I kept getting calls from lunar landscapers, comet cleaners and insurance agents. I just couldn't get anything done."

Captain Asher looked closely into D7's eyes.

"Really, it's true." D7 turned away. "Or my name isn't D7."

"Okay." Captain Asher had no reason to doubt D7. She had personally programmed her never to tell a lie. There was no way she could have known that the Buttermans had deleted the word *never* from D7's memory.

"See, Mom," Pokey said. "I told you there was an explanation. Can we go now?"

"One last thing."

"Aw, Mom." Pokey expected to get a good-bye kiss. He closed his eyes and grimaced. Then, instead of a peck on the cheek, he felt a slight pinprick above his shirt pocket. He looked down to see his mom pinning her wings on his chest.

"Have a good trip"—his mom saluted— "Captain Pokey."

Pokey saluted back. "Thanks, Captain Mom."

Captain Asher turned and walked off the *Meatloaf*.

"Close hatch," Pokey ordered.

"You got it, Poke." Bianca pushed a button and the hatch started to close.

The crew could hear the chant of the crowd—"Chocolate! More! Chocolate! More! Chocolate! More!"—until the hatch sealed out the sound and the *Meatloaf* was on its way.

Seven

Captain Pokey pushed down on the accelerator pedal. As his mother had before him, he pushed it until it almost touched the floor. The *Meatloaf* surged forward, quickly entering time warp and the space-time continuum.

A brilliant burst of light, like a million camera flashes all going off at once, filled the starship. The crew and company shut their eyes and covered their faces. Immediately all went totally black. It might have lasted a second, a minute or a million years, but in what felt like no time at all BB shook Ellie's shoulder. "Hey, El," he whispered, "I think we're home."

Moments later BB led the group off the starship. When he turned around to look at the mighty *Meatloaf,* all he saw was a rather ordinary-looking ranch house with a white picket fence. The ship's camouflage program and defense systems had automatically engaged.

"Why, hello, everyone," a familiar voice called out. "I knew you might have forgotten something and would have to come back."

"Mr. Mueller!" Ellie, BB, Joyce and Perry shouted simultaneously.

"Who?" Pokey, Bianca, Kurt and Connie asked in unison. They all had their hands resting on their phasers . . . just in case.

"How long have you been waiting?" Ellie asked.

"Oh, I'd say all of . . . ten seconds." Mr. Mueller smiled. "You just left."

Mr. Mueller was the cooking teacher at Rollindale School. He was from the year 6859. He had been sent back in time to help Project Ketchup succeed. Mr. Mueller also happened to be Captain Asher's grandson, which made Pokey . . .

"Hi, Dad," Mr. Mueller said when he was introduced to the sixth-grader.

"What?" The twelve-year-old Pokey looked suspiciously at the thirty-eight-year-old man.

"We'll explain it all later," Ellie said.

"Good idea," Bianca said. "We better get moving. We have to make a couple of meatloaves."

"And go chalklight shopping," Kurt added.

"That's *chocolate*," Connie corrected.

Now it was Mr. Mueller's turn to say, "What?"

"Same answer," Ellie said. "Later. Now, let's go."

As they walked, Bianca spoke into her communicator. "D7," she said, "aren't you going to come with us?"

"No, thanks," the android's voice answered back. "I have to wax the warp drive, and there are a couple of things I have to pick up."

About halfway to the candy store, Mr. Mueller disappeared.

B7 had watched and waited until everyone had turned the corner. Then she quickly reset the *Meatloaf*'s time coordinates to forty-eight hours ahead. She sat down in the captain's seat. "Dang those doughnut-holes!" she swore, seeing the empty ignition.

Pokey had taken his keys with him, and B7 had left her set in her other toolbox. That left only one course of action. "I guess I'll have to hot-wire it."

No one had *ever* tried to hot-wire a ketchup-class starship before, but being a machine herself seemed to help. B7, the former D7, had once rewired her own oil-digesting system and had rebuilt her left hand from scratch just for the fun of it. So, with a wire twist here and a laser connection there, the starship's engines soon fired up and the ranch house with the white picket fence took off.

Only a micromoment passed before B7 landed the house—same place, different time. When she popped open the front hatch, she saw Bertha and Beula sitting on the back end of a huge moving van. She also noticed that all the rear tires were completely flat, as if a great weight had squeezed the air right out of them.

Both Buttermans spoke with their mouths full of chocolate. They might have mumbled a greeting. It might have been a curse. All B7 knew was that the sight of Bertha and Beula's Butterfinger-filled mouths was disgusting, even to an android.

"You two are repulsive." B7 looked away.

"Thank you." Beula swallowed most of the candy bar, letting only a bit of Butterfinger juice dribble down her chin.

Beula and Bertha looked as if they hadn't shaved in weeks. But this time the problem wasn't whiskers, it was Whitman's and Hershey's and Nestlé and even a bit of Godiva. From their lips to their cheeks to their chins, they were a gooey mess of milk chocolate and dark chocolate.

"We were just finishing lunch," Bertha said while wiping her mouth on the back of her sister's dress. She reached into the truck and pulled out a box of Junior mints. "Want some?"

"Do you have anything with an oily center?"

"No."

"Then no, thank you."

"Your loss is my gain." Bertha patted her megadomed belly and wolfed down the mints. She went to wipe her hands on the back of Beula's dress again, but this time Beula was ready for her.

"Ah-ah-ah. No you don't." Beula turned around. "No more cleaning up behind my back."

Bertha wiped her hands down Beula's face, catching gobs of mint and chocolate on her bangs, eyebrows and bent and broken nose.

"That's more like it." Beula flipped her skirt and waddled off into the *Meatloaf*.

"Can you help me unload this stuff?" Bertha asked B7, pointing toward the truck. "That

Beula never helps bring in the groceries. Eat them—yes. Carry them—no." Bertha followed her sister's lead and huffed and puffed her way through the starship's door empty-handed.

B7 clicked her titanium-tipped tongue. "Some sisters," she snarled while walking to the truck. "Humans make the worst sisters. Give me a good vacuum cleaner any day. At least they have attachments I can borrow."

When she looked into the moving van, B7 couldn't believe her fiber-optic visual-reception units. It was jammed from top to taillight with chocolate. There were chocolate candies, chocolate cakes, chocolate pies—everything and anything that could be made of chocolate was sitting in the truck.

"Would you please hurry up?" Bertha stuck her head out a window. "We're getting mighty tired of waiting for you. We don't have all day, you know. Boy, you ask for a little help with the groceries and you have to wait forever. Sheesh!" Bertha pulled in her head and slammed the window shut.

"Even a pencil sharpener would make a better sister," B7 muttered as she pointed at the chocolate with her right arm. She pushed a button that was her middle knuckle. An amber tractor beam shot from her pinky, thumb and forefinger. It immediately enveloped the truck's cargo.

When B7 moved her arm, the several-ton mountain of chocolate floated out of the truck. She guided it to the "garage," the door to which automatically opened when the chocolate arrived. B7 slowly moved her arm so that the heavy, sweet load glided into the hold of the starship and gently settled to the floor. She put her hand in her pocket and cut off the beam.

The garage door slowly closed, and B7 joined the Buttermans on board the starship. She began to prepare for launch. "Destination?" B7 asked Bertha.

"Two-seventeen P.M. August second. 6689."

BB, Ellie, Pokey, Bianca and the rest raced back to the *Meatloaf* as soon as Mr. Mueller disappeared. They were worried about what they might, or might not, find. But when they turned the corner, everything appeared to be as it had been moments earlier.

A familiar, smiling android greeted them at the door. "Back so soon?" she asked. "Is there a problem?"

"Maybe a big one," Pokey said. "Hurry, D7,

we've got to get home now. Something has gone wrong. Start emergency launch sequence Macaroni Macaroni Macaroni and Cheese.''

"Don't we sound official?'' The android's voice had changed its tone. "Mr. Bigshot Human Captain knows his macaroni,'' she said snootily. "That's really using the old *noodle.*'' She tapped Pokey on the head. It hurt.

"Are you okay, D7?'' Pokey pulled out of tap range.

"Of course I'm okay. Couldn't be better,'' the android snapped. "In fact, I'm a lot better than any of you puny humans will *ever* be.''

Everyone looked at D7.

"What?'' The android threw up her arms.

Pokey silently noted the need for D7 to get a complete oil change, lube job and attitude adjustment as soon as possible. "Nothing,'' Pokey said out loud. "Let's fly.''

Within moments the starship and everyone on board returned to the future. But the future they returned to was nothing like the one they'd left behind.

Eight

When they raised the *Meatloaf's* hatch, the passengers' and crews' eyes popped wide open. The landing area was completely deserted and covered with long cracks and deep crevices. The starship's left landing pad had just missed a pothole that was deep enough to have flipped the entire spacecraft on its side. Weeds and grass sprouted tall through the breaks in the concrete.

It looked as though no one had bothered to maintain the spaceport for a century. "What happened?" a shocked Kurt asked.

Even Connie couldn't come up with an answer to her brother's question. Pokey was equally at a loss for words, and Bianca looked confused and more than a little scared.

On the other hand, BB, Ellie, Joyce and

Perry knew exactly what had happened, or at least who was responsible. One look at the stat- ues erased all doubt from their minds.

The statues stood about twenty feet from the starship. They were the chiseled figures of two enormous women; one of them had a huge mole on a rippled chin, the other had one stick- ing out of the middle of her forehead. Each held what looked like trays of desserts in their mam- moth arms. The words CHOCOLATE RULES were etched on the pedestals, and the names QUEEN BERTHA and QUEEN BEULA were inscribed on their respective bulging bellies.

"They did it," Ellie said while she, BB, Joyce and Perry pointed at the statues.

Bianca let out a little scream when she looked where her four new friends pointed. "Who are they?" she asked as she and her three class- mates took a step back. "They're so scary . . . and ugly."

"They're Buttermans." The android stepped into the open doorway to the *Meatloaf*. She spit oil, growled and let out a computerized belch.

"*The* Buttermans," two voices snarled from behind the starship. At first the faces behind the voices remained a mystery. Then the mystery was solved. Two gigantic shadows emerged from around one end of the *Meatloaf*. Then two almost-as-big Buttermans followed in their footsteps. They spit, growled and belched. "We're bad." Spit, growl, belch. "And you're busted." Spit, spit, spit, spit, growl, growl, belch.

As captain, Pokey knew exactly what calm and rational course of action was needed. *"Run!"* he yelled. *"Run fast!"*

No one was able to run quite fast enough. As the crew and company scattered in eight different directions, seven blimplike human forms materialized around them. The group was surrounded on three sides, with the starship blocking the fourth.

Kurt and Connie couldn't stop in time and ran headlong into two tremendous tummies. They felt themselves being engulfed by flesh before they could put their sneakers into reverse. All the others stopped running and fell back, repelled by the smells that now encircled them.

"You remember our cousins Babs, Baxter, Betina, Bruno, Brenda, Boris and of course Brumhilda, don't you?" Bertha asked.

"Nice to see you again." Brenda put out her hand to BB.

Bertha slapped it down. "You are all under arrest."

"What's the charge?" Bianca demanded.

"Don't sweat the small stuff," Betina laughed. "Trust me, you're guilty."

"Everyone into the starship," Pokey ordered, but the android was blocking the way. "D7," he said. "Help us."

"That's *B*7." The android gave her right cheekbone a twist, which turned her smile into a snarl. "And you are now officially Butterman bait."

Again everyone tried to run. Perry, Bianca and Joyce headed to the right and ran directly into a fleshy wall of Butterman flanks. They hit Bruno and Boris at full force, but the Butterman cousins didn't budge. The three would-be escapees bounced back as if they'd hit a particularly bouncy trampoline.

Kurt, Connie and Pokey ran straight ahead but fainted after inhaling the aroma of sardines, cigar smoke and stale elephant sweat that seemed to ooze through the air around Betina and Brenda.

BB and Ellie ran to the left but stopped just before they got to Brumhilda and Babs. BB had an idea. He reached into his pocket, his fingers finding what they were searching for. "Gum, anyone?" BB pulled out a piece of smushed bananaberry bubble gum.

"Pick me! Pick me!" The two Buttermans moved in closer.

BB smiled. "May the best Butterman chew." He threw the gum over their heads.

"Mine!" Babs and Brumhilda both shouted as they dived backward for the gum. They both hit the ground and started rolling down the runway.

BB and Ellie broke through the gap in the Butterman line and dashed off before any of the other cousins could react. They didn't stop running until they were a half mile away and standing in front of the banquet hall they had left less than an hour ago.

The hall was empty and looked deserted. Ellie pointed to a sign on the door. 75TH ANNUAL MALTED MILK BALL. RESERVATIONS REQUIRED. INQUIRE WITH IN.

Under that was another sign, this one in handwriting. *Mr. In is out. All inquiries will have to wait until Monday. Gone Eating!* Seeing as how it was still only Saturday, BB and Ellie decided that the banquet hall looked like a good place to hide.

When they were safely inside, Ellie noticed that BB was crying. "Don't worry," she comforted her friend. "We're safe, and we'll get the others out, somehow."

"It's not that," BB sniffled.

"Then what's wrong?"

BB wiped away two tears. "That was my last piece of gum."

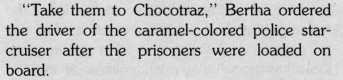

"Take them to Chocotraz," Bertha ordered the driver of the caramel-colored police starcruiser after the prisoners were loaded on board.

"What's Chocotraz?" Joyce hoped that Pokey or one of the others from the sixty-eighth century would answer her question, but they just shrugged and shook their heads.

Beula, on the other hand, leaped at the opportunity. "Oh, you'll find out what Chocotraz is," she sneered, and snarled. "You'll really, really, really find out. Oh, yes, you will." Beula paused and turned to her sister. "They will, won't they?"

"Yeah." Bertha grinned her semitoothless grin. "They'll find out."

"Told ya so. Told ya so."

Bertha leaned into the starcruiser and shouted into the driver's ear, *"Lock them up, and swallow the key."*

"Are keys good?" Beula asked. "If they are, can I swallow it?"

Bertha ignored her sister and slammed the starcruiser's door.

The trip to Chocotraz prison took only a few minutes, but in that time the prisoners saw what a century of Butterman rule could do. Half of the buildings that had been there earlier that day were gone, and those that were still in place looked as though they might collapse at any moment. The land below was littered with candy wrappers, cake boxes, Fudgsicle sticks and slime.

There were skyway billboards everywhere reading HAVE A SWEET LIFE, CHOCOLATE—THE MOST IMPORTANT MEAL OF THE DAY and REMEMBER— HEALTHY EATERS GO TO JAIL!

There were also floating TV commercials for shows like *Balloon Up with the Buttermans, Queen Beula's Beauty Tips* and *Queen Bertha's Bonbon Breakfast Club.*

"Who are those people?" Pokey asked.

Joyce and Perry told the entire terrible Butterman tale. They wrapped up just as the starcruiser entered the gates of what had to be the biggest, filthiest floating prison this side of the Milky Way.

"When did they build that?" Perry asked.

"I have no idea." Bianca couldn't believe her eyes. "It wasn't here an hour ago."

Regardless of its age or origin, Chocotraz prison was now very, very real. The huge metal gate slammed shut with a loud clang as soon as the starcruiser passed through.

The first stop was the registration and examination center. The sixth-graders were shocked at the size of the guards, the doctor and the nurse who waited for them there. They all weighed at least four hundred pounds, and the only thing worse than the condition of their skin was the crabbiness of their dispositions.

"Line up, you cabbagehead losers," the fattest guard barked, causing three brass buttons to pop off his pants and hit the guard by the door. As they were taking her to the hospital, the 422-pound doctor walked slowly in front of the students. He stopped for a moment before each one to scan him or her with a tiny device that had the words MINI MEDI-VEGGIE ELIMINATOR 5 on its side. When he pointed it at each person, a loud alarm sounded.

When the doctor was finished, he turned to his nurse. "This is worse than I thought. Every one of them has eaten vegetables, bread, meat and . . ."

"No!" All the guards gasped.

"Yes . . . *fruit,* within the past twenty-four hours."

There was a rumble through the room. Two guards spit in disgust, two others moaned in disbelief, and when the nurse heard the news, he actually started to weep and bang his head against the wall.

"Not to worry." The doctor was not only large, he was in charge. "Bring out Big Bertha."

"Yes!"

"Hooray!"

"You're brilliant!"

"A genius!"

The remarks and applause came from all sides. Only the prisoners were silent. The doctor blushed, shuffled his feet, lowered his gaze and said, "You're right. Do go on."

After another five minutes of meaningless compliments, the nurse pushed a button next to the door. Within seconds two prisoners, in uniforms with wide chocolate stripes, rolled in what looked like a King Kong version of the scanner that the doctor had held in his hands.

In honor of the queen the doctor had written the name BIG BERTHA on the side, above the machine's real name: MEGA MAXI MEDI-VEGGIE ELIMINATOR 6. The prisoners placed the thing on the floor and ran out of the room. The doctor turned it so that its front end faced the students.

Pokey, Bianca and the rest found themselves looking into a gaping black hole filled with spinning, swirling silver-and-pale-blue stars. When the doctor pushed a button, the stars shot out of the machine and circled the midsections of each student.

It really tickled. The stars danced on, over, around and through their stomachs before returning to Big Bertha. It was then that the students felt the pangs of hunger from their now completely empty stomachs.

The doctor peered into the unit. The stars were now bright red and lime green. "Just as I thought," he sighed. "This unit will have to be scrapped. We'll never be able to clean out that much real food."

"What about the prisoners?" one of the guards asked.

All six twelve-year-olds held their stomachs and groaned in pain. They had never felt so empty or hungry in their entire lives.

"Fill them with sugar." The doctor wrote down his prescription. "And take them to the movies."

Nine

Ellie and BB waited an hour, then an hour more. For quite a while they could hear Buttermans slowly rumbling by, each grumbling about having to search for the escapees while the Queen B's got to inspect the Chocolate Mint and the CIA (the Caramel Improvement Agency). All the Buttermans loved watching them print milk- and dark-chocolate money, and they were all interested in how the CIA was coming along in its efforts to come up with a caramel apple—without the apple.

None of the Buttermans checked inside the banquet hall. They didn't want to have to walk up the seven steps that led to the door. Eventually all was quiet and the ground stopped shaking.

"Where to now?" BB whispered.

"Let's head back to the *Meatloaf*." Ellie peeked through a window to make sure it was safe.

"Good plan," BB said. "What do we do when we get there?"

Ellie kept looking outside. She didn't say a word.

At the Chocotraz Cinema 7, the exact same picture was playing on all sixty-seven screens. *Night of the Living Buttermans* was produced and filmed by Historically Correct Productions, and claimed to be the true story of how the Butterman Empire came to be.

During the previews for films entitled *Beula Eats a Bavarian Chocolate Buffalo* and *Beauty and the Bertha,* the prisoners were brought in and seated in the first row. Each was given a tray filled with candy of all kinds. There were bars, bags and boxes filled with jelly beans, peanut brittle and chocolate with the coveted Buttermans' Best rating.

"Eat, eel-noses," a rotund guard ordered. "Eat now!"

"And what if we don't?" Bianca pushed her tray away.

Another guard wheeled in a brand-new Mega Maxi Medi-Veggie Eliminator 6. This one was nicknamed Big Beula.

"Then"—the guard patted the machine— "we just put this baby in reverse."

Bianca pulled her tray closer. "What can I say, except *bon appétit.*"

While the guards watched and drooled, the prisoners dug in and the lights dimmed. Moments later the feature presentation started to roll. The first thing the prisoners saw was the huge head of Beula on a lion's body. She roared a roar that proved she was queen of the beasts. Everyone cringed in their seats, but the Beula beast was just the start of something even more frightening.

The screen quickly turned dark. A voice came on. "What you are about to hear and see is true. This is history . . . according to the queens."

The scene cut to a close-up of Beula's and Bertha's faces. The prisoners jumped in their seats and gave out little screams.

Bertha cleared her throat. "The Buttermans rule . . ."

". . . an introduction," Beula finished.

"On three," Bertha said.

"One . . ." Beula paused.

The pause lasted until Bertha rolled her ruby-colored eyes. "Two, you beetlebutt."

"I would have remembered that if you'd given me the time." Beula looked a little embarrassed. Then she smiled and looked back over her shoulder. "Do you really think I have a beetle butt?" she asked hopefully.

"The camera's on . . . ," Bertha said through gritted and gapped teeth.

Beula smiled sheepishly. "Sorry." She paused and thought. "Oh, yeah: Two . . ." She snapped her fingers. "Three . . ." She tapped her toes. "Go."

The Buttermans started a new version of their old war chant:

"Some people used to fear us . . .
Said we're nasty and obscene.
They called us crooks, dorks, pimple poppers
and all things in between."

The Buttermans started to dance happily around the screen while they continued their chant.

"Bertha, Beula, quite contrary,
dirty, rude, unsanitary.

Just like Curly, Moe and Larry . . .
Awful! Ditzy! Dumb!"

Beula spun into a microphone operator, sending him flying across the set and into a year's worth of traction.

"If you believe that we're quite snotty . . .
uhhh, stick your toes right in the potty.
We ain't nuts . . . not even dotty.
Loony. Wacked. Or bummed."

On the screen, both Buttermans stopped dancing and faced the audience.

"If you still don't love us,
if you still think we're so mean,
all we can say's tough cookies . . .
'Cause, baby . . . we're the queens."

The Buttermans wrapped up their chant in the traditional way. They spit, growled and belched.

"We're Buttermans . . ."

Spit-growl-belch.

"The Buttermans . . ."

Spit-growl-belch.

"We're bad . . ."

Spit-growl-belch.

"So bad."

Spit-spit-spit-spit-growl-growl-belch.

Bertha and Beula winked at the camera. Beula's eyelid stuck to her eyelashes. As the introduction faded, Bertha could be seen trying to pry her sister's eye open. She could be heard screaming at Beula to remember to wipe *all* of her face after lunch.

Kurt and Connie put down the crunch bars. They'd had enough candy. The guard turned the Big Beula machine, already set in reverse, so that they could see the dark caramel-colored stars inside. Both resumed eating as the main part of the movie began.

The ditsy documentary started with a shot of the *Meatloaf* landing. The date August 2, 6689, appeared on the screen and, two seconds later, disappeared. Bertha, Beula and B7 walked out of the starship, which had the name

Milkshake written on its side where the word *Meatloaf* had been. The wild shouts of a crowd, which the announcer said numbered in the trillions, greeted all three Buttermans. They each held candy bars up over their heads, causing the crowd to go even wilder with gluttonous glee.

"We come with chocolate," Bertha announced.

The unmistakable shrieks of "Hooray!" "Yippee!" "Yahoo!" and "Make them queens!" burst forth.

"Wait a minute." Bianca stopped chewing a peanut butter cup. "If they just arrived, how does anybody know what chocolate is?"

"Look." Pokey pointed to various spots on the screen where Butterman cousins could be seen holding cue cards. They tossed out candy to those who shouted the words on the cards, and wrote down the names of those who didn't.

The moviegoers also noticed that the landing area where the *Milkshake* touched down looked a lot like the one where they had landed a few hours earlier.

"Guard, when was this low-rent movie filmed?" Bianca asked.

The guard nearest the machine turned on Big Beula. The caramel stars surrounded Bianca's belly, which she felt filling like a balloon. "All right, I'm sorry." Bianca batted at the stars. "I meant to say, when was this wonderful, great, glowing piece of art created?"

The guard turned off Big Beula.

Bianca felt as if she had eaten enough sweets to put even her most oinkish Halloween pig-out to shame.

The movie continued with still photographs and what looked like home videos of healthy-looking people. Some were thin, some were a little chunky, but all looked happy and well.

"This is the horrible condition of humanity before the arrival of the Chocolate Age," the announcer announced. "Here you see the same people during the first year of Queen Beula's and Queen Bertha's careful, thoughtful, kind and benevolent guidance."

The same people were shown wolfing down chocolate, devil's food cake and hot fudge sundaes. Bertha and Beula were smiling in the background. Actually, Bertha and Beula *were* the background.

"Citizens before the Buttermans . . ." the announcer said as the original shots of the people popped onto the screen.

"Citizens after the Buttermans." This time a group photo of the people was shown. It had to have been taken from a helicopter hovering way up in the air to have gotten them all in the shot. Each now weighed at least two hundred pounds more than they had before.

"Beautiful, just beautiful." The movie cut to a close-up of a tearful Beula. She blew her nose on her sleeve.

The film quickly cut through everything that had happened since 6689. It started with the Buttermans handing out sweets to the demanding crowd. Then it shifted to the sisters being declared queens, as long as they kept up the supply of chocolate, which they claimed to have invented. The announcer explained how, with their Starship *Milkshake,* the Buttermans could travel anywhere in time, which was how they were able to quite literally squash the Great Carrot Rebellion of 6701 almost before it started. Because of their time travel, the voice said, the Buttermans knew that the future would be bright beyond anyone's dreams as long as they stayed in charge. The Butterman sisters' message was simple and to the point: *If you want chocolate . . . you do what we say.*

The film told how, within a few years of the Butterman regime, the world pretty much started to be run on chocolate. Not only was chocolate the main meal, it also made up two of the Buttermans' four main food groups. The other two were sugar doughnuts and whipped cream. Any food that didn't fit into one of the groups was declared inedible and illegal to even lick.

The economy was moved to the chocolate standard, with every coin chocolate-coated and every dollar dipped in a different kind of chocolate, depending on its denomination.

The final scene showed Bertha and Beula neck deep in an Olympic-size swimming pool filled with thick liquid chocolate. As they started to walk up the pool's steps, the guards turned the projector off. Even they felt that having to see any more would be extremely cruel and hideously unusual punishment.

BB and Ellie had no trouble getting to the *Meatloaf,* but as soon as they opened the door and walked inside, B7 pounced like a mechanical mountain lion. She grabbed both students by the collars.

"So nice of you two to drop in." She sounded like the spitting image of her big human sisters.

B7 lifted BB and Ellie up in the air and

dropped them to the floor. She scooped them up and prepared to do it again, when Ellie noticed a small sign on B7's forehead. It was right above the rim of her bifocal alpha-spectrum video-modification enhancement visor. The sign read: IN CASE OF EMERGENCY—BREAK GLASSES.

Ten

Bianca, Pokey, Kurt, Connie, Perry and Joyce were all taken to a large holding cell with thick candy-cane bars. There were places where the red lines on the bars were gone, which served as memorials to those who had tried to lick their way to freedom.

No one had ever escaped from Chocotraz. By the time they were able to dig a tunnel or break off a bar, they were usually too fat to fit through the openings. Those who weren't were just too exhausted from their sweets-only diet to carry out their plans.

After being force-fed a lunch of baklava and sugar water, the prisoners were finally left alone.

Bianca spit the remaining pieces of the sweet treat from her mouth. "What's back-lava?"

"Baklava," Perry corrected. "It's a Greek dessert."

"Okay," Bianca said. "What's a Greek?"

Perry's answer was interrupted by Kurt's moaning. "Who cares? What do we do now?" He held his aching belly.

"You're such a baby," Connie moaned just as loudly, and held the same part of her body.

Bianca and Pokey were at a loss for a plan, but Joyce and Perry had a suggestion.

"Let's just wait for BB and Ellie," Perry said.

"They'll save us?" Joyce said.

Perry gave her a dirty look.

"Oh, I mean, they'll save us!" Joyce corrected her inflection.

Pokey shook his head sadly. "I really don't think they can do anything."

"Then"—Perry smiled through his stomach pains—"you don't know them."

Ellie didn't know exactly what would happen if she followed the instructions on B7's forehead. Looking down at the floor of the starship, she did know that she had no choice but to try. Before the evil android could continue to play

Drop the Students, Ellie took the glasses by the horn rims.

"No!" B7 shouted.

"Let's try *yes*," Ellie said calmly as she smashed the glasses against B7's iron-alloy left ear. They shattered into about a jillion and a half pieces, which sprinkled down onto the floor.

A low moan, a high whine and a most unpleasant hiss came from deep inside the android. Diamond doors closed over her ears, her eyes slammed shut with two loud bangs and her nose turned upside down and sneezed out billows of green smoke.

B7's arms slumped down, lowering Ellie and BB safely to the floor. A second later the android whirled once to the left, twirled twice to the right, did a spectacular jump, spin, double back flip and curled up in a corner.

"I think you broke her," BB said.

"You know, that could be us." Ellie pointed to the steaming wreck that had been B7.

"I'm glad you broke her," BB said.

"Me too," Ellie agreed. "Now we can use the starship to find the rest of the guys and get out of here."

"I think you missed one teeny tiny detail," BB suggested.

"What's that?"

BB gestured all around the starship. "We don't know how to work this thing."

"Okay," Ellie said a bit defensively. "But that's only *one* teeny tiny detail."

"If only we had D7 back," BB said. "Then we'd be cool."

Ellie's eyes lit up. "BB?" she said.

BB mistook Ellie's look of excitement for one of anger. "I'm sorry. I know we can't get D7 back. We don't know how to fix a toaster, much less rebuild an android. It was just a stup—"

"You're brilliant!" Ellie shouted.

"Stup—endously brilliant, idea of mine." BB covered his tracks. "Why don't you tell me what my plan is . . . just so that I can see if you really understand."

Ellie held up the bent and broken frames she had in her hands. "Here's the secret."

BB looked even more confused than he had during last week's math test. "Exactly," he said. "Go on."

"It's so simple."

"That's the beauty of it." BB had no idea what Ellie was talking about.

94

Ellie looked at the android. "I wonder if she has an extra pair of glasses."

"Who cares?" BB huffed. "Tell me the plan."

"That *is* the plan."

"You're right!"

"Quick," Ellie said. "Help me look for them."

"For what?"

"The glasses."

"You're right again!"

Ellie started going through drawers, cabinets and proton storage chambers.

"Just as a test," BB said while looking behind the star-sensor unit, "tell me what good it would do if we found them. Wouldn't it just mean that she would come back to life?" BB pointed to the mangled mechanical mess in the corner. "She wasn't in a great mood when you broke her; I'd hate to be around after she's fixed herself." BB paused. "I mean, I just want to hear how you'd answer that kind of question. If I really asked it . . . which I didn't."

"Yeah," Ellie said while searching under the antimatter pods. "Maybe she'd come back mean . . . or maybe all she needs is a new prescription."

BB got it. "Or an old one? Like before the Buttermans messed her up?" He smiled.

"Exactly." Ellie continued the search.

"You're right," BB said.

"About what?"

"I am kind of brilliant. You know, like an Alfred Einstein."

"That's *Albert*."

"Oh, yeah, like you're all of a sudden the brilliant one." BB smirked.

Ellie was in no mood to argue. She and BB searched the entire starship before finding what they were looking for under the android's combination bunk bed and tool table. Ellie held the metal case, which was labeled D7— VIDEO-MODIFICATION ENHANCEMENT VISORS—ALPHA SPECTRUM—SHADED. She quickly opened it and looked inside.

"Sunglasses?" BB laughed. "An android with sunglasses."

"Well." Ellie smiled. "She used to be one cool machine."

Ellie pulled the visors from their case and walked across the starship. After turning B7's nose back to nostril side down, she carefully put the visors in place.

A deafening grinding sound filled the starship . . . followed by a whistle, a roar and the sound of a robin chirping. The android leaped to its feet. "Hello, BB. Hello, Ellie. As you say in your ancient language . . . what is up?"

"*D7?*" Ellie said slowly.

"In the metal."

"You're back!" BB shouted.

"From where?" D7 asked. "And why am I wearing my sun visors?"

"Don't you remember anything?" Ellie asked.

D7 quickly scanned her newly restored memory banks. In the flash of a laser disk and the blink of an eye, it all came back to her. The Buttermans, the reign of chocolate, the breath of the one called Beula the first thing in the morning. D7 shuddered. "How embarrassing," she said. "Those Buttermans really tapped into the dirty, dark side of the—"

"Of the force?" BB asked.

"No, of the neuronetwork microchips I've been meaning to wash. But they're dry-clean only, and who has time? I mean, I barely have a moment to—"

"I think we can worry about your laundry later," Ellie said. "Right now we have to save Joyce, Bianca and the others."

"No problem," D7 said. "I'll just beam them back here."

"Where do you think they would have taken them?" BB asked.

D7 again ran a quick reverse scan of everything her bad self had learned. The blueprints for Chocotraz projected out from her right eye and onto the far wall of the starship.

"On second glance," D7 said, "I think we might have a very big problem."

"What's wrong?" Ellie looked at the image on the wall.

D7 held out her right hand, and a purple laser pointer shot from her pinky. She circled the prison with the pointer. "Chocotraz is surrounded by a force field made up of microscopic Gummi Bears."

"So?"

"Did you ever see someone who's been beamed through Gummi Bears?"

Ellie and BB couldn't say that they had, but they could imagine that it would be quite a mess.

"Can we eat our way through?" BB suggested.

"It would take too long." D7 shook her head. "And it would be bad for your teeth."

"So, what do we do?"

"There is one place where the prison might be somewhat vulnerable."

"Where's that?" BB asked.

D7 moved her pinky so that the pointer pointed directly at the middle of the diagram of Chocotraz. "Its soft center." D7 retracted the pointer. "It might be gooey, but it's our only hope."

Eleven

BB and Ellie were chin deep in cherry cream. D7 had managed to beam them through a pinhole-size opening in the Gummi force field that was located directly above the prison's soft center. The prison builders needed the opening for ventilation and figured that no one in their right mind would try to beam into, or out of, that chamber. BB and Ellie were fast coming to the opinion that they were right, and that D7 had to have more than one screw loose to have come up with this plan.

The cavern they were in was as big as a domed football stadium, and it was usually filled to the ceiling with sugary goo. D7 knew it was only drained twice a day, at noon and midnight, to supply the prison's dessert factory and to replenish the Buttermans' private stock. It was now 12:03 P.M., and the cream was once again starting to rise to the top.

"Let's get out of here!" BB yelled.

"Over there." Ellie raised her arm out of the glop that had now reached lip level. "See, it's just where D7 said."

BB looked where she was pointing. He saw the ladder leading up to a trapdoor halfway to the roof. He suddenly thought of a question he wished he had asked before beaming in. "What if it's locked?"

"Then we're candy filling," Ellie said as she and BB slogged through the sugary swamp to the ladder.

Ellie led the way up. They both felt globs of cherry cream dripping off their clothing and skin as they pulled themselves out of the muck. They climbed up rung after rung on the ladder, while the cream rose inch by inch after them.

BB and Ellie almost slipped at least a dozen times. Their cherry-coated hands had a tough time getting a grip, and they had to fight to keep their feet from sliding off the rungs. More than once Ellie's foot slipped and landed on BB's head. It left a hot-pink footprint right in the middle of his hair.

"Watch where you're stepping!" BB shouted.

Ellie looked down and couldn't help laughing. "I think footprint-pink is your color. It looks so natural."

BB kept climbing, swearing silently to himself to shave his head as soon as they got home.

Twenty rungs up the ladder, the climbers realized that they still had twenty-five to go before they would reach the door. As the cherry cream dried on their skin, instead of being slippery, their hands and feet started to feel as if they were coated with glue.

"Let's rest a minute." Ellie breathed heavily.

BB looked down at the ever rising glop. "I think we better make that half a minute."

The rate at which the chamber was filling had increased dramatically. Instead of rising one inch for every step BB and Ellie took, it was now rising at three inches per rung, and the pace continued to quicken.

The two rested for fifteen seconds before continuing the climb. The slime now approached at five, then six, then seven inches for each step. Finally Ellie reached the door. She turned the handle and pushed with all her might. The door wouldn't budge. She pulled harder than she had ever pulled before . . .

nothing. "You're right!" Ellie screamed down to BB. "It's locked!"

BB could think of only one thing to say. "Keep climbing!"

Ellie took her friend's advice. They climbed higher and higher as the gurgling glop started lapping at the laces of BB's sneakers. "Look," Ellie cried out. "Another door!"

Sure enough, not twenty feet up, about three feet from the ceiling, another door jutted out slightly to the left of the ladder.

"Better hurry." BB kept pushing upward but could feel the cream starting to ooze into his high-tops. "And the hurrieder the better."

Not ten seconds too soon, Ellie reached the door. *"BB!"* she screamed.

"Oh, no, is it locked?" BB yelled as the cherry cream surged up the legs of his jeans.

"I don't know."

He felt it reaching his knee. "Umm, maybe you should, like, try it?"

"I can't."

"Why?" Over his knees and up his thighs, the gickey mess rose.

"There's no handle."

BB looked at the door. It was smooth and, as reported by Ellie . . . without a handle. He groaned as the cream filled his belly button, moaned as it reached his neck, and silently screamed as it covered his mouth, nose, eyes and head.

Just as BB was about to give up and kiss his sweet self goodbye, he felt himself being yanked upward. It was not a soft yank, and the hands doing the yanking were harder than stone. "D7!" BB cheered when his head cleared the surface, causing creamy chunks of cherry stuff to spray from his mouth and shoot out of his nose.

BB's eyes cleared just enough to watch D7 closing the door against the rising flavor-filled ferment. He saw Ellie panting in the corner a few feet away. She was coated with cream up to her cheekbones. Both tried to clear their eyes, noses, mouths and minds of what had just happened.

"Okay, enough fun," D7 said matter-of-factly. "I think we should rescue now."

"F-F-F-fun?" Ellie stammered angrily. She pointed toward the now-closed door. "You call what happened in there fun?"

"Yeah," BB said, feeling sick from all the cherry cream he had just swallowed. "We were almost cherry cordials."

"Nonsense." D7 checked her internal Rolex.

"Everything's right on schedule. In fact I saved you with .021956 seconds to spare."

"Oh, wow," Ellie said sarcastically. "If we had known that, we would have stayed for tea."

"You are such a wartworry." D7 smiled and patted Ellie on the shoulder.

"You mean worrywart." Ellie moved away.

"Whatever you like. Let's go."

As they walked out of the small room and started down a winding staircase, BB asked D7, "How did you get in with the guards all over the place?"

BB and Ellie watched D7's electronic expression go from friendly to fierce.

"What?" the android screamed. "How dare you question *B*7's ability? I'll have you turned into Butterman bars for this, you Twinkie-toed turnip-muffins!"

Ellie and BB were ready to run in the opposite direction when *D*7's warm and welcoming personality returned. "Impressive, if I do say so myself," she said. "It's a good thing I took that acting program last summer. The guards just thought it was me, as *B,* instead of me, the *D.* They weren't about to ask any questions."

BB and Ellie remembered their friend's recent fierce face and also decided against asking questions—just to be on the safe side.

D7 smiled. "It should be a Simple Simon rescue from here on. I gave the guards around the holding cell the day off to celebrate the queens' birthday."

"Is it the Buttermans' birthday?" BB asked.

"In this century," D7 said, "every day is a Butterman birthday. Come on." She gestured the group forward. "Let's be heroes."

The prisoners sat in the cell, staring at the walls. Only Perry stood at the bars, trying to nibble his way out.

"BB! Ellie!" Perry screamed as soon as he saw his friends round the corner.

Pokey had covered his face with his hands. "Don't waste your breath yelling. They can't hear you," he said sadly.

"Oh yes they can," a familiar computer-generated voice said cheerily. "Their audio receptor-percussion devices are in fine working order."

"D7?" Pokey spun around in the air. Bianca jumped up and down. Kurt and Connie hugged each other briefly before wrestling each other to the ground.

"Flee now—fight later," D7 advised the twins while breaking the lock with one hand and opening the cell door with the other. "Here, everyone, put these on."

D7 pulled butterscotch-colored devices from a drawer in her left hip. They were each made of two doughnutlike circles, connected by a hard toffee chain. D7 noticed the confused expression on every human's face as they looked over the devices. "They're candy cuffs," D7 explained. "Put them on your wrists. If we run into any guards, we'll pretend you're my prisoners."

"Why didn't we get in that way?" BB still felt the squish of cherry cream in his shorts.

"Wouldn't have worked. The Buttermans have spies everywhere. They would have reported us before we even got in the gates. But this way, we should be able to waltz right on out of here before anyone has time to report anything."

D7 patted herself on the back for her knowledge of ancient sayings, while all eight young people snapped on their cuffs.

"One question before we go," Bianca said.

"Yes."

"What's a waltz?"

D7 didn't know it, but once again two pairs of beady, puffy, bloodshot eyes were watching their every move. While she'd been in the starship, new, invisible video scan units had been installed all around the holding cell.

The Buttermans had big-screen monitors put in every room of their palace so that they could keep an eye on the prisoners and watch cable wherever they went. Beula's favorite dinner music channel was M&M's TV, while Bertha favored the beat on We Ate 1. While today's programming had nothing to do with music or munching, the Buttermans were glued to the screen.

"Waltz on out, will they?" Bertha snarled and grabbed Beula by what hair remained on her head. "Come on, sis." She dragged Beula out of the room. "We're going to the dance."

"Wait! Stop!" Beula yelled as she felt one of her last patches of hair being pulled from her head. "I don't have a thing to wear."

Twelve

D7 led the way. Her bad self, B7, had entered a blueprint of Chocotraz into her memory banks, so even though she had never been there, D7 knew the place like the back of her microcircuits. She remembered every nook, cranny and tickle-'em-till-they-talk interrogation room.

Without hesitation D7 walked ahead of the group. She made six lefts and thirty-two rights, went up sixteen staircases and down three, and through sixty-three doorways and one large plastic tube.

Chocotraz was designed like a Martian maze to prevent escape. One wrong turn or step would land the escapee-wanna-bes in a vat of fast-drying chocolate super goo. They'd be stuck there until the Butterman cousins ate them free and returned them, bite marks and all, to their cells. After that experience, no prisoner had ever tried to escape twice.

D7 pointed to a door at the end of a very dark hallway. She checked her internal map and announced happily, "That's it. We are out of here."

Neither D7 nor the students had noticed—although they should have. No one had paid it the least bit of attention, even though it should have sounded a loud and strong warning. The escape path had been too clear. It was as if someone wanted them to reach the exit door unchallenged. Not a single guard or prison worker had tried to stop or question them. In fact, all the way from the cell to the exit door, they hadn't seen, heard or, in the case of the Buttermans, *smelled* anyone. As soon as they opened that final exit door, they found out why. The Buttermans had given all the rest of the guards a half day off . . . without pay. When the door opened, the escape route had closed—blocked by a barricade of beefy Buttermans.

"Going somewhere, my little SweeTarts?" Bertha Butterman smirked. "Going somewhere special?"

"Excuse me, sis," Beula whispered in Bertha's ear. "I think they were trying to escape. I think that's where they were going."

"I know that, beanobrain," Bertha whispered back. "Don't you recognize sarcasm?"

"Where is it?" Beula looked wildly around. "Can I eat it? Is it good? Can I—"

Bertha thwacked her on the upside of her down-covered forehead, causing her sister to shift subjects.

"—spaghetti and beetballs?" Beula completed another thought that had nothing to do with the subject at hand.

Meanwhile, the prisoners and the android had another thought of their own. They slammed the door shut, locked it and ran back inside. Again, D7 confidently led the way. She wasn't about to share the news that flashed from deep within her circuitry as they headed away from the door. Chocotraz prison had only one way out, and that had been it.

"I thought *you* had *your* keys!" Beula whined after Bertha ordered her to unlock the door.

"You borrowed my keys when you went to lunch yesterday, dim-doodle," Bertha yelled.

"Oh yeah? Then where are they?" Beula secretly remembered that she had placed her sister's keys just a bit too close to her hot fudge sandwich, and that they had accidentally become the most nutritious part of the meal.

Bertha's eyes narrowed and she spoke slowly. "Did you eat them?" Bertha knew her sister very well.

"Ummmmm," Beula stalled, feeling a heaviness in the pit of her stomach that might have come from nervousness, or from Bertha's keys.

"You did eat them!" Beula shouted. "Give them back now!"

Bertha forced open her sister's mouth with her left hand and attempted to retrieve her keys with her right.

Fortunately for Beula, Babs Butterman took matters into her own flab. She interrupted the operation by ramming her hefty hip into the four-inch thick, triple-reinforced, Dolarian-diamond-plated Saturnian-steel prison door. The door didn't stand a chance.

Babs stood over the fallen door and motioned her cousins through. "After you, my dearies." She quickly changed her mind. "On second thought . . . after me."

Babs led the Buttermans over the door in pursuit of the prisoners. Only Bertha and Beula stayed behind as Bertha tried to remove her fist from her sister's throat.

Babs knew Chocotraz prison well. It was one of her favorite vacation spots. She found the view of the bars and all those unhappy faces "quite refreshing." She led the Butterman brood up to the nearest prison computer nerve cluster.

"Hi, Penelope." Babs had become close friends with the prison computer. They were on a first-name basis.

"Hello, Babs, dearest," the computer answered. "Your hair looks lovely today. Did you have it done?"

Babs fluffed the blond hair that sprouted from the mole on the lower left side of her nose. "No, I just blew it dry this morning."

Next to Beula, Babs had the most magnificent mole hair in the entire family.

"Well, whatever you're doing"—the computer's voice sounded both synthetic and sappy—"keep doing it."

The other cousins groaned with envy as Babs exhaled heavily through her nose, causing the hair to wave in the breeze. Penelope kept talking. "This is really a very pleasant surprise. I didn't expect to see you until three A.M. Remember, we're supposed to wake up all the prisoners for a surprise Tootsie Roll call. It should be quite the giggle."

Babs smiled at the thought but quickly brought herself back to the business at hand. "Penelope, I need a favor."

"For you, gorgeous, anything."

Babs blushed and blabbered on. "We have some prisoners who are trying to escape."

"Oh, I'm sorry I didn't notice. I was on a lubrication break. Did they fall into the chocolate pits?"

"I'm afraid they're not in the pits. And they won't *be* in the pits."

"Why not?" Penelope asked. "Everyone who tries to escape ends up in the pits."

"Not these prisoners," Babs said. "D7's leading them."

The computer's tone went from satin smooth to razor sharp. "Don't you mean *B7*?" Penelope snapped. "I never trusted that old bucket of bolts."

Penelope and B7 had never gotten along. She was jealous of the android's relationship with Bertha and Beula as well as of the fact that B7 had legs.

"B7 is now D7," Babs said. "And she's helping the new prisoners escape."

"I knew it! I just knew it!" Penelope's lights

were flashing wildly, particularly the red ones. "I warned the queens about that Ms. Dandy Disks. I told them that model was known to turn on its owners. I told them so, but did they believe me? A tabletop unit? No, I tell you. No no no no no no no no."

"You did tell them." Babs tried to comfort her friend.

"It's gotta be the legs," Penelope huffed. "It's just gotta be."

"And now you can get even with her." Babs snickered.

"Can I have the legs?"

"And the arms and the ears, if you help us find them."

"With extreme pleasure." Penelope scanned every inch of Chocotraz. "Corridor three, section twelve, deck sixty-six, unit nine. They're heading for the dessert factory."

"You're a dear." Babs patted Penelope on the control panel. "There'll be extra chips in this for you. I guarantee it."

"Chips ahoy!" Penelope dismissed the offer. "I want her belly button too, and I want it bad."

"It'll look good on you," Babs called over her shoulder as she and the cousins stampeded toward the door.

While Penelope searched her circuits for the

best place to put a belly button, the Buttermans stormed out of the room. Babs and Boris tried to ram through the open door together, which resulted in a much bigger opening than had been there before.

The Buttermans charged, ran and barged onward until they were halfway to the dessert factory. Then they all collapsed in one enormous mushy heap.

Their sugar-based diet had completely zapped their energy reserves to the point where they went from being filled with adrenaline and spite, to becoming stone-cold, empty and exhausted. The Buttermans had fallen to the floor and could not get up.

Meanwhile, Penelope was too busy concentrating on finding the right site for her new navel to have noticed the collapse of the Butterman brigade. Her navel maneuvers were only interrupted when Bertha and Beula rolled into the room. "Report or be Penelope unplugged," Bertha ordered.

After being told that everyone was heading for the dessert factory and being asked for their belly-button placement opinions (Beula thought it would look wonderful between Penelope's DE-LETE and ENTER buttons . . . Bertha didn't care), the queens took advantage of their regal positions. They called to the palace transporter operators with their jeweled communicators.

"Royal beam-out," Bertha ordered. "Prison dessert factory. And hurry."

Bertha turned to Beula. "We'll wait for everyone there." She smiled a mean little smile. "It should be quite the party."

"I still don't have anything to wear, and you said it was a dance, not a party," Beula whined as she and Bertha disappeared and were transported on their private beaming channel directly to the factory. They arrived inside just as Ellie, Bianca, BB and the rest raced down a narrow hallway and reached the outside of the factory door.

This time Bertha waited for the group to walk all the way through the door before issuing her greeting. Perry was the last one through. He looked back to see if any Butterman was gaining on them before shutting and locking the door. "All clear," he happily reported. "Not a buttfaced Butterman in—"

Just then Bertha and Beula stepped out from behind two 700-million-gallon pots used to melt down and make various chocolates for the royal treasury. "Hello, my little trufflemakers." Bertha grinned. "May I be so bold as to say . . . *Gotcha!*"

"Umm." Perry stumbled toward the door with the rest. "Can I, uh, take that 'all clear' back?"

Bianca quickly clicked the lock and threw open the door. One look down the hall showed that the only escape route now was blocked by crawling Buttermans. Babs was first in line. Like a person dying of thirst in the desert, she cried out for what her body desperately needed. "Pasta. Pasta," she moaned before falling down in a sugar-induced state of total exhaustion.

Bruno was right behind her. "Baked beans. Baked beans."

He was followed by Brumhilda. "Kumquats. Kumquats."

"Kumquats?" Everyone looked at Brumhilda, who just shrugged and sagged over on top of Bruno, crushing him to the floor. Butterman collapsed on Butterman until the hallway looked like the mouth of a cave . . . after a cave-in. It was solid wall-to-wall, floor-to-ceiling Buttermans, with no room for even the ghost of a fashion model to squeeze through.

BB, Pokey and company turned and faced Bertha and Beula. D7 walked out and stood between her friends and her enemies. She got down on her knees and started to cry.

hirteen

"You ruined my surprise," D7 sobbed. "Ruined it. Ruined it. Ruined it!"

Everyone from Beula to BB had a confused look on their face. Ellie tried to comfort her kneeling comrade. "Don't cry, D7. It's not over yet." She gave the android a hug.

D7 broke free with such force that it threw Ellie halfway across the room, where she landed bottom down on a pile of rock candy.

"Get away from me, nosedrip," the android roared. "And stop calling me names. It's not nice."

For a moment Ellie thought D7 was joking, but the pain from her bruised backside countered that argument quite effectively. "That hurt!" she complained.

"Too bad." The android copied Ellie's voice exactly.

"*B7?*" Beula started to approach the android, but her sister yanked her back by the nape of her monstrous neck.

"Not so fast," Bertha warned. "Remember, we watched her free the prisoners and act a lot like, excuse my language, *D7.*"

"That was my surprise." The android resumed her sobbing. "I pretended to be Ms. Goody Two-footpads so that I could get them all in here together. I wanted to give you a surprise present of chocolate-covered students."

"That's so thoughtful." Beula broke away and handed the wailing android a moderately clean hanky. "Stop those tears before you rust or short out or something."

Bertha still wasn't about to bite the bait. "Okay, she said suspiciously. "If you really *are* our B7, and that was your plan, I only have two words to say to you."

"Goody, goody?" Beula offered.

"No," Bertha said. "Try *prove* and *it.*"

"*O* and *K,*" the android sneered. She pointed her right ring finger at the group of students. She went from person to person before pausing and pointing directly at BB.

BB was about to discuss the impolite nature of pointing when a violet-and-yellow teleporter beam shot from the android's fingertip and covered him like a banana in a bowl of Jell-O. Did he see her wink? He wasn't sure. All BB was certain of was the fact that he was being lifted high into the air. He heard his friends yelling *"No!"* and saw them rushing the android. As it turned out, they were a bit late.

BB looked down and saw that he was over one of the chocolate pots, and then the beam vanished. BB felt himself falling. Then all he saw was brown, and all he tasted was sweet.

Within a second after the android had turned off the transporter beam, there was a loud gurgling noise from the pot. Then the sound of machinery. Not a second and a half later, a door opened at the bottom of the pot. There was a loud burping sound, and a very large piece of chocolate candy was spit out onto a conveyer belt.

Bertha and Beula started to laugh and clap their hands. Ellie, Pokey and their friends started to scream in horror. The candy had the soles of two cherry-stained high-top sneakers sticking out of one end and the marking BB swirled on the top.

"B7!" Beula and Bertha oozed their way over to the android. "You're back!"

The two sisters gave the android a big greasy Butterman hug. One hugged from the right, one from the left. They squeezed so hard that the android popped up from between them like a hot dog squeezed from a mustard-filled bun. The android flew ten feet straight up before turning on her foot jets and lowering herself slowly to the ground, outside of the hugging pair, who failed to notice that the object of their affection had been ejected from their embrace.

"Um, hello. I'm out here," the android said, tapping Bertha on the shoulder.

"So you are," Bertha said. There was an audible peeling-away sound when the sisters separated. It was like the sound a person makes when getting up from a plastic chair while wearing shorts on the hottest day of the summer.

"You are a dear." Beula closed her eyes and moved to once again hug the android. She missed and ended up hugging a small bulldozer, but she didn't seem to notice the difference.

"What now?" the android asked Bertha.

"I say we continue along with your surprise," Bertha said thoughtfully. "It was such a delicious idea."

"You mean—" the android started to say, but was interrupted by Bertha's giggle.

"Indeed I *do* mean." Bertha looked at the prisoners and happily said, "Let's make some candy."

Beula ambled over to the conveyer belt and took a lick off the top of the BB-filled chocolate cluster. "Do it, B7," she laughed. "Do it to all of them. Right now."

"Your command is my wish." The android pointed the index fingers of both hands at the prisoners. Before they could dive for cover, purple-and-yellow beams shot out from under her nails. But this time, when the beams got halfway to their targets, they disappeared. The android blew on her fingers and put her hands into her side boxes.

"Why did you stop?" Beula cried.

"Answer her." Bertha lowered her eyebrows, which made her look like a demonic bulldog after a biscuit binge.

"Well," the android teased, and shifted her weight from one leg to the other and back again. "I could dip them all right now . . ."

"Yeah-yeah-yeah-yeah-yeah-yeah!!!!!" Beula clapped and slobbered.

"Or . . ."

"Or what?" Bertha barked.

"Or, I could let *you* do it."

"Me-me-me-me-me-me-me!!!!!" Beula spun in circles.

"Wait," Bertha said. "We ain't got no beam."

"No," the android agreed. "But you do 'got' arms and hands."

"You mean *push* them in?" Bertha's brows and spirits rose.

"It is a much more hands-on approach," the android pointed out.

"And so much more fun." Bertha spit out each word, along with enough saliva to irrigate a small field.

"To the top!" The android pointed to a huge metal stairway that circled the pot and led up to a platform at the rim.

"Beam us up, B7," Bertha and Beula said at the same time. They laughed with pure joy at the thought of what was about to happen.

"Can't do it," the android stated. "My finger beamers can't take the weight, and the palace transporter operators are at lunch."

Bertha and Beula stopped laughing. "Then how do we get up there?" they asked together.

"Climb."

"Climb?" Bertha and Beula gasped as one. "Queens don't climb."

"I'll let you stir," the android said to tempt them.

"No." The Buttermans folded their arms and pouted.

"And lick the spoon."

"Okay." The Buttermans nodded and grinned.

Spoon licking was one of the Buttermans' favorite activities. In fact, in the sixty-eighth century they had declared it an Olympic event.

The android turned to the prisoners. "You first! Up the stairs!"

"And just what if we say *no?*" Bianca challenged.

The android pointed a pinky at the bulldozer that had recently been the object of Beula's affection. A green beam shot out, and the machine vaporized.

"Up is good." Bianca, her friends and the android started up the steps with Bertha and Beula in very slow pursuit.

With every step the Buttermans took, the stairway groaned and swayed. Several steps actually broke and fell to the factory floor below. The prisoners and their mechanical captor were happy to safely reach the top while the Buttermans were still only halfway up. At least the platform wasn't shaking, rattling and threatening to roll off its moorings and crash to the ground.

After many dangerous moments the Buttermans managed to huff, puff and bellyache their way to the top platform. When they got there, they counted kids and found one missing.

"Where's that punk named Pokey?" Bertha demanded.

"I'm so sorry," the android said. "I couldn't resist. I didn't think you'd miss just one."

"But he was such a good one!" Bertha screamed.

"You might still be able to see him sink."

The sisters used the last of their breaths and energy, and raced to the edge of the platform. They looked down into the vat of swirling chocolate.

"I don't see nothing," they both said.

The android joined them and leaned over as far as she could. "There's the head," she said matter-of-factly.

"Where?" Both Buttermans leaned over as far as they could. Then they leaned forward a bit more. This presented the remaining prisoners with the biggest, roundest, most irresistible targets they had ever seen.

"I think I see some hair," Beula said excitedly

as D7 stepped aside and nodded to the prisoners, who immediately took action.

Ellie, Joyce and Kurt simultaneously rammed their shoulders into Bertha's backside. Bianca, Perry and Connie did the same to Beula. The Buttermans teetered, tottered and finally tumbled off the platform.

A moment later there was an incredible double splash, and the students and the android found themselves drenched by a chocolate tidal wave. No one had time to celebrate the victory. The pressure of having supported the Buttermans and the chocolate backwash after their fall were too much for the platform to bear. It ripped away from the pot, sending everyone flying through the air.

D7 set her index fingers on extreme wide-angle beam, ignited her maneuvering thrusters and hoped for the best. It worked. The students did somersaults, dances and fancy flips as they were slowly lowered to the ground in a beautiful blue tractor beam. When they reached the factory floor, they were greeted by Pokey and BB.

"Yes!" Ellie screamed as she ran up to BB and gave him a big hug. She quickly punched him in the arm to counter the embarrassment caused by her show of emotion.

Everyone had watched D7 transport Pokey to

safety as the Buttermans huffed their way up the steps, but the last time they'd seen BB, he was still a chocolate-covered peanut.

"What happened?" Ellie asked.

"Simple," D7 said. "I picked BB to chocofy because I knew that he would be the only one who would be able to—and actually want to—eat his way out."

"It was delicious." BB licked his fingertips. "I think I'm my favorite candy."

Just then a low moaning sound came from the pot. The sound grew to an earsplitting shriek. Then the sides of the pot started to split open.

"Duck!" Bianca yelled.

Everyone dived behind a vat of liquid marshmallow fluff as the chocolate pot exploded.

When the smoke cleared and they looked up, they saw the two biggest chunks of chocolate Butterman clusters in the history of humankind. One hand, a foot and a nostril protruded from one candy. An entire nose, a bit of belly and a few stringy hairs of unknown origin could be seen sprouting from the other.

Suddenly an angry munching sound could be heard from inside the chocolates.

"Quickly," D7 said. "We have to start the conveyer belt."

Perry ran to the control panel next to the sagging belt that held the Buttermans. The others lined the sides of the belt. D7 quickly stuck a straw into each of the three visible nostrils and said, "Now!"

Perry pushed the button marked START. The belt moaned, groaned and failed to move. The chomping sound was getting louder and closer to the surface. The people on either side of the belt grabbed hold of it and pulled with all their might.

Perry pushed OFF, and then ON again. The pulling was just the boost the belt needed. It started moving slowly toward what looked like a giant car wash. As the Buttermans started to go into the machine, BB and the rest could hear them growling. When they were all the way inside, D7 ran to a panel, flipped a switch to HEAVY and pushed a button marked SPRAY.

A fine mist, then a torrential downpour of colored liquid sugar, filled the machine. When the Buttermans emerged from the other side of the device, the sounds of munching were gone and they were covered with a hard candy shell.

Fourteen

It took some doing, but they did it. The eight young humans and their friend, D7, managed to roll the Buttermans out of the factory and all the way into the Starship *Meatloaf*. More importantly, they did it without breaking the breathing straws or cracking the shells.

Pokey, Bianca, Kurt, Connie and D7 took their places at the various control panels and prepared for launch. BB, Ellie, Joyce and Perry struggled to strap in the Buttermans before taking their passenger seats and making sure their seat belts were securely fastened. While the *Meatloaf* warmed up, everyone stuck on their time displacement patches.

"What about them?" BB pointed to the red-and-blue-shelled Buttermans. Faint eating noises could once again be heard beneath their hard surfaces, and little stress fractures had started to appear on the shells. "Should we give them patches?"

BB looked at Pokey, who looked at Bianca, who looked at Ellie. Everyone looked at everyone else. There was a long pause before everyone said, "Nah!"

Pokey floored the *Meatloaf* and left a trail of burned ions in its wake.

When they opened their eyes they saw they were circling Earth. The time-continuum analyzer showed they had arrived back at the time when ketchup was a condiment and chocolate was just candy.

Because of its cloaking screen, no one noticed when the ranch house with its white picket fence landed halfway up the block. As soon as the starship was secure, the crew threw open the screen door and stepped outside. They immediately knew that their mission had been a success.

Mr. Mueller was back, and he was coming up the walk. "Hi." He waved. "What's up?"

Pokey raced out of the starship and hugged Mr. Mueller with all his might. He looked up at his son and smiled. "You exist again!" He laughed. "You really exist again."

"Boy"—Mr. Mueller looked down at his twelve-year-old father—"I knew I was feeling a little funny awhile ago, but I thought it was just a cold."

Suddenly Pokey's family reunion was cut short by the loudest, most grating, monstrous, bansheelike cries anyone had ever heard. It sounded like a werewolf-Bigfoot with ten stubbed toes and a mouthful of aching wisdom teeth.

"Um, excuse me, everyone." D7's voice boomed from a loudspeaker. She had stayed behind in the *Meatloaf* to make sure everything was turned off. "I think you all better get in here in a hurry. It's the Buttermans . . . they've hatched."

When everyone ran inside, they were greeted by the sight of two very fat, very bad and very, very loud babies. They were tangled up in two soiled black dresses that looked big enough to be the tents at an evil circus.

There were pieces of candy shell everywhere, although all the chocolate that had coated the grown-up Buttermans was gone. When the babies saw the crew, they screamed even more loudly.

"I'll tell you one thing." Mr. Mueller covered his ears against the beastly babies' cries.

"What?" Pokey shouted up to his son.

"Those two babies really need to be changed."

"But who's going to do it?" Ellie asked.

Mr. Mueller volunteered to do the job. "The first thing we do to change these two is put them on a diet."

The Butterman babies wailed more wildly than ever. Mr. Mueller placed one squirming bundle of blubber under each arm and headed out the door.

After gathering together a dessert tray to make any baker or candymaker proud and picking up a few books on the problems that too much of a good thing can cause, it was back onto the *Meatloaf* for the passengers and crew.

In no time they had taken off, and landed in the same spot. Only five thousand years had flown by.

As soon as they unsealed the hatch, the time travelers heard the huge crowd chanting and cheering, "Chocolate! More! Chocolate! More! Chocolate! More!"

Captain Asher raced onto the *Meatloaf* and saluted her son and his friends. According to her time-continuum wrist analyzer, the starship had returned exactly fifteen seconds after it had left.

"All I can say," Captain Asher said as she winked and tasted a Twinkie, "is—what took you so long?"

About the Author

Jerry Piasecki is the creative director for a Michigan advertising agency. Previously he was a radio newsperson in Detroit and New York. He has also written, directed and acted in numerous commercials, industrial films and documentaries. The writing he loves most, though, is for young readers, "where one is free to let the mind soar beyond grown-up barriers and defenses." Jerry lives in Farmington Hills, Michigan. He has a teenage daughter, Amanda, who has a dog named Rusty and a cat named Pepper.